CANDLELIGHT REGENCY SPECIAL

CANDLELIGHT ROMANCES

Bride
of a
Stranger

Lucy Phillips Stewart

A Candlelight Regency Special

Published by
Dell Publishing Co., Inc.
1 Dag Hammarskjold Plaza
New York, New York 10017

Dell ® TM 681510, Dell Publishing Co., Inc.

ISBN: 0-440-10808-X

Printed in the United States of America
First printing—November 1979

Bride
of a
Stranger

Chapter 1

At one time Adrianna would have shrunk from the prospect so clearly in store for her, but the years had taught her that happiness for the orphaned daughter of an impoverished peer was rarely to be found. She had dreamed of so much more from life for herself, and wondered whether she could abide the reality of the loveless marriage that had been forced upon her. Thought by her relatives to be very fortunate to have been offered for by the Earl of Ravisham, she might have welcomed the match had she had any say in the matter. As it was, she was dispirited, but determined not to give way to the despondency threatening to engulf her. Leaning back against the comfortable padded squabs, she sighed inwardly and refrained from peeping at the Earl seated beside her in the light traveling coach.

No one could deny that he was handsome. From

his carefully brushed, windswept hair to the toes of his gleaming Hessian boots, he presented the very picture of a notable Corinthian. Adrianna deduced that he was tall. At least it had seemed so when he had stood beside her to repeat his wedding vows. Beyond this, she had had but the haziest impression of a classic profile and the weary disillusion in a pair of gray eyes.

His voice was heard beside her, speaking lazily, "You do not object to driving rather fast, I trust. It is quite safe; my coachman is familiar with this road."

She was taken off her guard and said, glancing at him, "It is not my custom to raise objections, whatever I may think."

He seemed not to notice the bitterness in her tone. "I fancy you may be feeling some slight irritation of the nerves," he remarked, regarding her keenly. "In the months ahead, I will do my best to allay your fears."

She looked startled. "I thought—I was under the impression that—you would not be overly desirous of my company."

His smile banished the serious expression from his face. "I beg you will tell me why you thought that," he replied in a carefully pleasant voice.

She colored slightly and said, "I cannot conceive what could have induced you to offer for my hand."

"There is no understanding it at all," he agreed, a twinkle in his eyes.

She directed a sharply suspicious look at him. "Surely you knew my history. My father—"

"Are you apprehensive that he would have forbade the marriage? I sincerely hope not."

"He would have been delighted. And why not? There is, after all, the disagreeable stigma of poverty attached to my name."

"Don't talk nonsense, my dear. Many another girl has been left penniless."

"And therefore ineligible, sir."

"The relatives with whom you have been forced to live put that notion into your head. What did they say about me?"

"It wasn't very flattering," she chuckled, her spirits rising. "They cast you as being abominably affectatious in your dress, addicted to pugilism, curricle-racing, and gambling; all the vices, in fact, of a rake."

"Admitting to jealousy would be, of course, bad ton."

"I should rather think it would. The thought of my elevation to a position in society superior to their own was hard to bear. And to make matters worse, the marriage settlement was of a generosity to baffle their understanding. It baffled my own, I might add."

"Why? Did you expect me to settle a mere pittance on you?"

"I have had every opportunity over a period of years of inuring myself to the economies of poverty, my lord. It would have worked no hardship on me."

"It would have on me."

She was spared the necessity of answering by the horses' slackening pace and, glancing out of the window, saw that night had fallen. It was impossible to discern much of the country through which they were passing, the moon being behind the clouds; but the horses soon slowed to a walk, and the vehicle turned off the main road onto a gravel drive. It was immediately seen to be ill kept, for the coach bounced through a number of potholes before drawing to a standstill before the door of a rambling house. The groom jumped down from the box, the steps were let down, and the Earl handed Adrianna to the ground. The moon chose that moment to illuminate the scene, and Adrianna found herself staring in disbelief at a ramshackle building of considerable size. Shutters hung drunkenly from many of its windows, and the limb of a large tree, sheared away from its trunk in some long-forgotten storm, lay across the shattered remains of one tall chimney pot. The flower beds had gone untended, and the shrubbery was overgrown by the encroaching wilderness.

The groom had tugged at the bell some moments before, and after an interminable wait, the door was opened by an elderly retainer in rusty black livery with tarnished silver buttons. "What be ye wantin'?" he demanded, favoring the groom with a melancholy stare.

The Earl, mounting the front steps by Adrianna's side, swore softly under his breath. "I am the Earl of Ravisham," he said. "Why is the house in darkness, and what do you mean, appearing before us shabbily dressed?"

"There be no cause for ye to talk that way,"

came Chittering's surprising reply. " 'Tain't no one here but me and the Missus. Everyone else done left long ago. We does the best we can, but ye won't find Twinfriars much to yer likin'."

This sage observation proved only too true. The main salon was discovered to be a large and drafty apartment, with magnificent oak paneling sadly in need of polish, a vast fireplace across one end of the room which had blackened the ceiling with its smoke, and an expanse of dusty flooring from which a tattered carpet had long since been removed. Long brocade draperies, once very elegant, were now faded and threadbare; a large oak refectory table standing in the corner of the room, bearing a pair of tarnished brass candlesticks, was covered with a thick film of dust; several chairs, one of them with a broken leg, were drawn up willy-nilly before the fire. Numerous paintings of dubious artistic merit covered the walls and were festooned with cobwebs.

Adrianna's astonished gaze moved over the room, coming to rest presently on a tray forgotten on a chest, and bearing, in addition to a jug of cream turned sour in the heat, a pot of cold tea and a bowl of pottage with fat congealed on its surface. Something in the sight, coupled as it was with the appalling dilapidation of the entire property, put her in mind of her relatives' irritation at her sudden ascent to a position of great wealth. Her eyes began to dance. She said in her most pleasant tones, "Twinfriars is not, I trust, your family seat."

It seemed to her that a faint look of surprise

flickered for a moment in his eyes. It was the first time he had heard her speak in a voice much above a whisper. He replied coolly, "I believe an exact enumeration of my resources was explained to you before you accepted my offer of marriage."

She looked startled. "I believe it was," she said, coloring slightly at the falsehood.

"It is not my intention that you should labor under any misapprehension. I have not seen this depressing real estate before in my life." His contemptuous gaze swept the disordered room as he spoke, and then returned to a contemplation of her countenance. "We will go elsewhere."

She hoped that she succeeded in preserving her calm. "The hour grows late, my lord. If you can tolerate it, I can."

He bowed slightly. "Since you wish it," he said.

She did not wish it, but the alternate prospect of driving on to seek other lodging after their exhausting day appealed to her even less. She said, somewhat doubtfully, "Perhaps when a meal has been prepared, and the beds aired—"

"From what we have seen thus far, I shouldn't pin my hopes on it," he remarked with a touch of amusement in his tone.

She could readily believe this. Detecting his rather heightened color, she realized—tardily—his own embarrassment. Feeling at a loss, she said cheerfully, "I will waste no time in seeing the house put to rights. If you will ring the bell, I will instruct the servants in their duties."

"It would seem I have taken an optimist to

wife," he remarked, tugging at the bell-pull. "It is very probably broken."

"Very probably. How could you have let the property fall into such an appalling state of disrepair?"

"I have only just inherited it. Great-uncle William was an irascible old rascal, and something of a recluse. I was brought up on tales of his oddities."

"I daresay he was touched in his attic."

"He was related through marriage, thank God. You needn't worry it will affect the descent."

She blushed to the roots of her hair. "If you will excuse me, sir, I—"

"Don't be a prude!" he interrupted, with another glance of dislike around the room. "I had the cork-brained idea of stopping here to inspect the place on our way to—" he paused and glanced at her "—my family seat. Forgive me. I had not at all expected Twinfriars to be so—"

It was her turn to interrupt. "I am sure I am at a loss to understand how anyone could have expected it," she said in rallying accents. "Well, it would appear the bell-pull does not work. Do open the windows and light a fire while I see what can be found in the kitchens. I doubt if there is so much as a crust of bread in the house, but we shall see."

"You appear to be not at all what I expected," he remarked, his eyes roaming over her face.

"Did you expect me to enact a tragedy for all the world like some foolish heroine found between the covers of a penny novel?" she asked, beginning to enjoy the situation. "Not a bit of it."

"No, so I apprehend. Does your courage ever desert you?"

"Only rarely," she replied, moving toward the door. "Pray do not purposefully burn the place down around our ears when you light the fire."

His smile gleamed. "It would solve my problem, however ineligible the act."

"However shockingly ineligible, sir," she said and left the room.

The Earl watched her go, then crossed to kindle a flame in the gigantic fireplace. Dubiously adding a log from the stack upon the hearth, he eyed the puffs of smoke issuing into the room and thrust a poker into the coals, scattering them and allowing the fire to go out. A search through the cupboards failed to turn up any candles other than tallow ones, so he put two of them into the tarnished candlesticks and lit them. The offensive odor that presently assailed his nostrils caused him to retreat into the hall in search of the kitchens, his footsteps echoing hollowly on the bare floors. Coming upon the taciturn retainer, he was forced to endure a few remarks on servants being expected to labor up stairs with blankets and cans of hot water before receiving the direction he sought. In the end he gave a few directions of his own and, turning on his heel, strode away to the kitchen door.

"Do look where you step," Adrianna cautioned him the instant he entered the room. "I hope you are fond of ham and eggs. And ale. There seems to be nothing else to drink in the house."

The Earl picked up the kitten at his feet and studied Adrianna from under drooping lids. "Cats and ale," he said. "Good God!"

"Mrs. Chittering is raising them," she explained, taking the ball of fluff into her own hands. "Their mother deserted them, poor dears. She has probably taken up with the stable tom."

"The candles send off a terrible stench, and the fire won't draw. Starlings are no doubt nesting in the chimneys."

"Well, there is no use making a fuss about what cannot be helped," she replied, crossing to restore the kitten to a box among its fellows, the hem of her gown picking up a great deal of dust in the process. "After we have eaten, I will see which bedchambers can be made presentable."

"Were you intending we swallow that?" he demanded, eyeing the ham on the table with distinct disfavor.

"It doesn't appear particularly palatable," she admitted, picking up a knife. "When I have cut away the outside, however, we should do quite well."

"I don't pretend to know why you think we should do quite well," he replied, taking the knife from her hand and laying it down. "You are coming with me," he added, seizing her wrist.

The entrance of Chittering caused him to release her. "All this comin' and goin'," the elderly retainer complained, crossing the kitchen. "First 'tis food, and now the horses to be put to, if ye please. 'Tis more than a body can stand."

With these words, and without paying Adrianna

17

and the Earl the least heed, he clumped across to the door leading to the stable yard and disappeared through it.

Adrianna turned a face of undisguised mirth upon his lordship. "I think it very probable," she said, "that no efficient servant remained for long in your uncle's employ. Chittering was doubtless used to be a stable-hand. I'm sure he would like to see the last of us."

"That is exactly what he is going to do," he replied, lips grim. "Where did you put your pelisse?"

"In the hall," she answered, ushered irresistibly through the door. "I thought you wished to inspect your property."

"My man of business must do so," he snapped, snatching up her wrap from the chair where she had laid it. "Put this on. We shan't remain a moment longer under this roof. What did you do with your bonnet?"

"But, my lord, where will we find to stay at this hour of the night? Are you acquainted with this neighborhood?"

"No, but inns abound in any place," he answered in much the same way he would have reasoned with a recalcitrant child. "You don't appear to trust me to provide for you."

"I didn't mean it like that," she said, flushing slightly. "Shall we go?"

After glancing at her averted face, he picked up her valise and his portmanteau and followed her out front. Neither of them spoke until the coach was brought around and he had assisted her inside. Spreading a rug over her knees, he expressed the hope that she would not feel chilled by the night air and took his seat beside her. The steps were put up, the door closed, and the luggage bestowed on the roof. In a few moments the coach moved forward, bowling along in a well-sprung manner until the wheels struck a particularly deep pothole. His arm was instantly about her shoulders, clamping her against his side until the vehicle ceased its rocking. She then expected him to release her, but he bent his head and pressed his mouth to hers. Stunned, she attempted to pull away, but he held her immobile, studying her keenly in the faint light of the moon filtering in, until his lips again claimed hers.

"No," he murmured, raising his head. "You are not quite what I expected."

She was wholly bewildered, and could only stammer, "I beg your pardon?"

"I said you are not what I expected."

"You are abominable," she uttered, jerking free. "What did you expect?" she couldn't stop herself from adding.

"A designing female," he replied with unimpaired calm.

"It is not surprising," she shot back, retreating to her corner of the seat. "I doubt you register any other kind among your friends."

"Very true," he said, favoring her with another of his measuring stares. "I required a wife; no female of my acquaintance could fill the bill."

"I think you must be out of your mind!"

"I am not. Neither am I trifling with you. Had

you turned out to be like others of your sex, I would not bother to be honest with you."

"If you could not be honest with other women, they were no doubt all either already married, or tarts!"

"You seem to have accurately divined the difference between yourself and them."

"Such assurances make this conversation no more acceptable, sir! It is, in fact, quite reprehensible!"

"It is also straightforward. I had need of a wife for several reasons, but mainly to beget an heir. I am the last male issue in my line. Should a fatal accident befall me, our name would die out."

"Your propensity for curricle-racing, I take it?"

"Quite."

"I still think you must be mad!" she said, maintaining her composure with a strong effort. "I could have been the wrong sort of woman to—to—"

"Be the mother of my children?" he finished for her. "I saw you first at a ball. When my interest continued upon subsequent sightings, I inquired into your reputation. No, you needn't glare. I cannot see your features clearly in this light, but I know you are. You will be in no worse case with me than with your relations, and my offspring will have a mother who is above reproach."

Much to her surprise, she found she was not at all shattered by his frankness. "Has it occurred to you that you have shopped around for a wife much as you would select a cravat?" she demanded, hardly knowing whether to feel amused or to feel cross.

"You know little of a gentleman's attire. Selecting a cravat is a serious business."

She was for a moment deprived of all power of speech but, recognizing his teasing, rallied quickly. "What if I had previously formed an attachment for another gentleman?" she said, thinking to best him.

To her chagrin, her sally fell wide of the mark. "You have not done so," he said. "When I kissed you, I knew that no other man before me had availed himself of the privilege. I will admit to being astonished. I shouldn't have thought it possible."

"Shouldn't have thought it possible!" she gasped. "Well! How am I to take that?"

"As a compliment. Beautiful girls usually become accustomed to being kissed immediately they leave the school room. You do not want for sense. Look in your mirror."

"I am not so set up in my own conceit as to wish to do so. However did we get off on this subject?"

"It was bound to come up. Unless you take to hiding your glorious hair under a turban, it must come up."

"It isn't glorious. I am a—a carrot-top."

"No. Fiery red perhaps, but a carrot-top? Never!"

She blinked. "Never?" she repeated, thrilled to be spoken to in such a way for the first time in her life.

"Never!" he corroborated. "As for your eyes, how can they be so blue? One feels that one can swim in them."

"Oh!" she breathed, turning her head to peep at him.

He burst out laughing. "Insatiable vixen," he said. "Your skin is flawless, and your figure, what I have seen of it thus far, appears to be magnificent."

She suddenly feared they were treading on treacherous ground, and changed the subject. "I am sure my relatives are relieved to have me off their hands," she said. "It cannot have been pleasant to have a penniless girl foisted onto them."

"You are well rid of them," he replied, perfectly willing to follow her lead. "I know what you have in your valise, my dear. A scullery maid receives better pay."

"What—did my cousin tell you?" she asked hesitantly, glad of the concealing dark.

"He didn't need to tell me anything. No lady would leave her wedding gown behind. Even the most insensitive dunderhead would know one valise could contain very little else. Your trousseau consists of the traveling costume you have on, and whatever falderals a lady considers necessary for her wedding night. Or do I stand corrected?"

She blushed to the roots of her hair. "You are aware of the—the cloud under which I went to live with my relations," she whispered after a moment. "I cannot find it in my heart to fault them."

"I thought we would return to that. What your father's financial losses have to do with you, I fail to understand. Not that it matters. I think you will find that your credit as the Countess of Ravisham will be all you could desire. Your relations will no doubt seek your good will."

"Oh, do you think so?" she said eagerly. "Nothing would give me greater pleasure than to snub them."

"It is a fortunate thing that you are not vindictive," he remarked, amused. "I would hate to live in constant fear of offending you."

"Odious man!" she declared, laughing. "If I have learned anything of you in the past two hours, it is that you will in all probability abuse me at every opportunity."

He groped for her hand and raised it to his lips. "You must know I have found no little delight in your company during those same two hours. I would that we could have become better acquainted before our nuptials took place."

"Why couldn't we have?" she asked, curious.

His eyes became veiled. "I had my reasons," he said briefly.

"My cousin termed it an unseemly affair, to marry in such haste," she said before she thought.

The Earl, having pondered and discarded the notion of confiding in her, put her off with a remark on the lack of sensibility inherent in her relations, and lay back, hoping to forestall further conversation in a like vein.

He was unknowingly abetted in this determination, however regretfully, by a party of young springs out for an evening of fun. Having been spectators of a horse race held in the district, they had topped off their day in a local pub, refreshing themselves liberally from the landlord's stock of ale. A curricle race down the center of the main highway resulted, accompanied by a great deal of shouting, singing, and laughter. The Earl's coachman, forced to the side of the road by the vehicles thundering down on him, did his noble best, but the right rear wheel went skidding down a steep bank, and the coach crashed onto its side at a crazy angle in a deep ditch. Inside, the Earl had clamped Adrianna to his side at the first sign of trouble, but they had been flung rudely over, with her body pitchforked atop his.

Outside, all bedlam had broken loose. The young gentlemen, sobered somewhat by the mishap, had drawn their vehicles to a standstill and had come running back to lend what assistance they were capable of. The coachman and groom, having had the foresight to leap clear, picked themselves up from the hedge that had broken their fall and struggled over to the coach. Forcing open the door, the coachman took in the situation at a glance. "Are you hurt, my lady?" he asked, reaching down a hand.

"No, not in the least," she replied, hoisting herself up with his assistance. "His lordship appears to have received a nasty crack on the head."

The Earl was indeed unconscious and had to be lifted out. The coachman climbed down into the coach and carefully handed his lordship through the door into the waiting arms of the groom. A moment later, the Earl lay stretched out on the verge beside the road, his white face clearly visible in the moonlight.

"Go to the horses' heads," the coachman told

Will. "You!" he growled at the shocked revelers. "Where is the nearest town?"

"There is a village a mile down the road," one of the youths hastened to answer. "It is small, but there is an inn."

Adrianna, who was on the ground by the Earl's side, collected her scattered wits. She said to the coachman, "His lordship must be tended by his own surgeon. Where is he to be found?"

"In London, my lady. I figure that Will can be there and back with the doctor by morning."

"Send him on his way at once. I am certain these gentlemen will wish to convey his lordship to the inn. I feel equally confident they will oblige us by affording Will the use of a curricle. Well, sirs?"

"I fancy it is the least we can do," the more sober of the young gentlemen replied.

"Then let us waste no more time. His lordship will catch his death out on this cold ground. Lift him carefully, now. You have done quite enough damage as it is."

Chapter 2

The village was indeed quite small, consisting of a few dwellings on one side of the road and the church and the inn on the other. Local wags, when in their cups, were fond of quipping that only a few steps separated Heaven from Hell in their part of the world. Adrianna, upon perceiving the inn, was inclined to agree. It was an unpromising hostelry, with a common tap room taking up the entire ground floor, and one bedchamber above. The kitchen and living quarters for the proprietor were, presumably, located in the lean-to out back.

The landlord, upon learning the identity of his injured guest, was obviously taken aback, but assured Adrianna that his lordship would be quite comfortable and led the way upstairs. Running ahead with the candle, she had scarcely time to turn back the sheets before the by now sobered revelers carried the Earl into the room and lowered him gently onto the bed.

"Get his boots off first," she instructed the landlord. "You will need to cut away his coat, it fits so snugly. One of you run down to the kitchen for a knife," she added, glancing at the youths. "The rest of you had better go."

"A sick room is no fit place for a lady," the landlord remarked, tugging at the Earl's Hessians.

"Pray concern yourself with his lordship's welfare," she replied, moving to the head of the bed. "I will not be in the way, I assure you."

"How did this happen?" he asked, removing the boots.

"There was never anything so disgraceful," she answered, smoothing the Earl's hair back from his brow. "Our coach was forced into a ditch by those young gentlemen. Have you laudanum in the house, in case his lordship stirs? I have sent for the doctor, but it will be morning before he arrives."

"I will see to it immediately we get his lordship between the sheets. I've seen worse raps on the head than this, my lady. It's you I'm worried about. Where will you sleep?"

"On a pallet beside the bed, if you will be so good as to make one up."

The landlord looked scandalized, but since the youth came into the room at this moment with the knife, he set about the task of slitting the seams in the Earl's coat, keeping his opinions to himself. While he and the young man stripped the clothing from his lordship, Adrianna busied herself smoothing his pillow, her eyes carefully no lower than his chest. Having done all he could for the moment, the landlord pulled a sheet up over his patient and hurried away, promising to procure the laudanum. Adrianna felt the Earl's brow and found it no longer cold. Satisfied, she sat down in a chair to await his return to consciousness.

A few minutes later he groaned and opened his eyes, his gaze finding her. "Has the surgeon been sent for?" he asked, shifting position slightly.

"Have the goodness to lie still," she replied, rising to her feet and crossing to the bedside. "The doctor will be here in the morning."

"I make you my compliments. There appears no end to your resourcefulness. I see my coat is ruined."

"Yes, I know. But it was you who brought us to this neighborhood, remember."

He made an effort to hoist himself up and sank back on the pillows, blanching. "The devil," he said, wincing. "I should never have sent my man on ahead, but I thought we would do better to spend our first night alone together."

Her eyelids flickered. "You will do yourself additional injury," she admonished, the pink tinging her cheeks.

"My dear, it is the veriest hurt. I have had worse. Be a good girl and send for a bottle of brandy."

She smiled, but her voice held no hint of laughter when she spoke. "Certainly not," she said.

The Earl, casting her one sharp glance, felt his soul stir. "I am accustomed to having my requests complied with," he said.

"That," she responded, smoothing his sheets, "does not altogether surprise me. In this instance, however, I will decide what is best for you. There now. Is that more comfortable?"

"Yes, thank you. Whether you approve or not, I will have my brandy."

She shook her head. "You will drink nothing but the laudanum the landlord is bringing."

He frowned. "You are mistaken, madam," he snapped. "I shan't swallow the damned stuff."

His head pained him, and he was cross. She longed to smooth the crease from his brow. "I am not mistaken," she said gently.

"May I ask," he purred, in deceptively silken tones, "how you propose to pour it down my throat?"

"I have only to hold your nose," she pointed out. "The landlord could contrive to keep you immobile while I do."

He regarded her silently for a long moment. "For the present it seems I must permit you to play the tyrant," he remarked with a flash of humor. "Make the most of it while you may. I will be on my feet tomorrow. Then we shall see."

"That will be for the doctor to say," she promised, a glint of amusement in her eyes.

"You are a remarkable woman," he informed her, "but I will not have you ordering me about."

Adrianna did not appear to be noticeably dashed. "I am sure I meant it for the best," she said, heaving a mournful sigh. "If I have been forward, my lord, pray forgive me."

There came a brief but pregnant silence. "I cut

my wisdoms years ago," he said. "You don't fool me in the least. Where are you going?"

"To fetch your laudanum, sir."

It proved unnecessary, for the landlord rapped at that moment and bustled in bearing a glass on a tray. "Here we are," he said. "Your lordship will rest that much better, once you have drunk this."

The Earl hesitated, but finally accepted the potion. Downing it, his eyes never wavered from Adrianna's face. "Satisfied?" he said, handing the glass back to their host.

"Completely," she replied, crossing to pull the curtains against the moonlight. "If you will be so good as to prepare a snack for me, I will appreciate it," she added, turning to the landlord. "Bread and butter will do nicely."

"If your ladyship will but condescend to a soft boiled egg, they were fresh laid just this morning."

Adrianna having agreed, he bowed himself out, promising to have the pallet made up shortly. She glanced apprehensively at the Earl, but he was already drifting into a laudanum-induced slumber and had missed the remark, much to her relief. She lost no time in going to bed herself. As soon as she had eaten the light repast, and the pallet was ready on the floor, she removed her gown and faced the choice between sleeping in her chemise or donning the diaphanous gauze nightgown. I may as well be comfortable, she decided, slipping the filmy garment on over her head. Softly tiptoeing to the bed, she stood gazing down at the Earl before creeping to her own hard pallet to compose herself as best she might.

She was awakened at an early hour by roosters crowing in the distance. Sitting up, she felt somewhat stiff, and startled, until memory came flooding back. Rising cautiously, she saw that the Earl's breathing was regular and his color normal, and crossed to dress, her back to the room. His lordship, opening drowsy eyes, found himself staring at an enticing view of a naked back. I wonder who she is, he mused, and then realized he had no memory of where he was, or even his own identity. I will sort it out later, he decided, and let his delighted gaze roam from her shoulders to her waist and on over rounded hips to long, slender legs. It's a shame to clothe such beauty, he thought, as she tossed the nightgown aside and reached for her chemise. The lids veiled his eyes at the first slight turn of her head, and to Adrianna, glancing uncertainly toward the bed, he lay to all appearances sound asleep. Cautious of making the least sound, she quickly dressed and went stealthily from the room.

Downstairs she partook of a breakfast consisting of ham and eggs, toast with its crust cut away (a touch the landlord assumed habitual with the Quality), and tea. She longed for a cup of coffee, or even chocolate, but thought it useless to ask.

The landlord, who had never before entertained a peer of the realm in his humble inn, slipped out the back door and went running across the field to a nearby farmhouse; presently the Widow Conway came hurrying up to Adrianna to discuss a diet suitable for an invalid. Both ladies possessing great good sense, it was immediately agreed that, while broth and a chicken wing might suffice for luncheon, by evening his lordship would be sufficiently recovered from the ministrations of the surgeon to demand a more substantial meal. Breakfast, however, was very much nearer at hand. By the time the doctor had arrived, Adrianna had somehow succeeded in spooning the contents of a bowl of bread-sops in warm milk down the Earl's throat. This drew a grunt of approval from the doctor, but not so much so as to permit her a place by the patient's bedside. He took off his coat, rolled up his sleeves, and ordered her from the room.

With matters now reposing squarely on her own shoulders, she went downstairs in search of the groom, locating him out front. "I know you have had no rest, Will, but Coachman has gone in search of a wheelwright, and there is no one else to send. Please go to his lordship's London home and inform the butler he is to dispatch a coach to us here to transport his lordship. I have no idea when the surgeon will permit us to leave this place, but I should think perhaps tomorrow."

The doctor, however, when he descended from the Earl's room, specified that his patient was not to be moved for two days, and then only a short distance, and in a conveyance traveling very slowly. His lordship had sustained a slight concussion and was to be kept quiet. Adrianna saw nothing for it but to return to Twinfriars.

As for the Earl, he was in too much pain from a splitting headache to object to the sleeping draught ordered by the doctor; he slept fitfully most of the day, and when he did stir he seemed comforted to find Adrianna sitting beside his bed. It was late afternoon before their wills clashed, the Earl having stated his intention of dressing and going downstairs, and Adrianna having just as firmly vetoed the idea.

"You try my patience!" he informed her explosively. "You will do very much better to refrain from telling me what to do!"

"If you would refrain from aggravating your condition, sir, there would be no need for me to do so," she replied, a dimple appearing in her cheek.

A vibrant stillness fell in the shadowed room. Adrianna demurely lowered her eyes to her hands lightly clasped in her lap, aware that words crowded together in his throat, none of them fit to be uttered in the presence of a lady. After a little while, he said stiffly, "My tone was rough. Pay no heed to it."

She lifted eyes brimful with laughter to his face. "I hope I have too much sense to be put out of temper by the things you say, much less by the manner in which you say them. By tomorrow you should feel much better."

That made him chuckle. "Not so naggy, in fact," he said.

"Not nearly so naggy," she agreed.

The smile left his eyes, and he gazed at her in a way she found distinctly disconcerting. "Who the devil are you?" he demanded suddenly.

She could only hope the dismay she felt did

not show on her face. "Feeling playful, are you?" she said. "In that case, sir, I feel under no obligation to cosset you."

"Oh, for God's sake," he uttered, half to himself. "You don't look like a nurse."

"Oh?" she murmured, perplexed. "What do I look like?"

"A mistress," he stated with decision. "Are you my mistress?"

"No," she replied coolly, maintaining her poise. "It seems perhaps a pity, but the fact of the matter is, I am your wife."

"The devil you say!" he muttered, frowning. "I don't know you!"

"No," she agreed. "We are virtually unacquainted."

His gaze traveled slowly over her face. "You could have done much better for yourself than to marry a stranger," he said at last.

"Since you seem to favor straight speaking," she snapped, eyes kindling, "I will inform you that no one but you appeared likely to escort me to the anvil."

"Forced into it, were you?" he mused, with a great deal too much perception for her peace of mind. "My good girl, why did you not inform me?"

"I had no wish to," she told him frankly.

"I would never have forced you down the aisle. At least I don't think I would have done. Are you with child? For if you are, and it is mine, yes, I would have married you out of hand."

She flushed to the roots of her hair. "Anyone

with a grain of tact would have left that unsaid," she told him severely.

"I presume from that that you aren't pregnant," he observed, noting her discomfiture. "Why did you marry me?"

"I don't expect you to understand, but Providence had decreed that I should have very little control over my own fate."

"I take it you think poorly of Providence."

"Very poorly, sir."

He sighed. "My head aches far too vilely for me to argue. I will only remark that it is not flattering to me to learn that my wife was forced into marriage with me by her relations."

"No, but the thing is, you angered me into admitting it."

"Don't quibble. Are you certain you are my wife?"

"Quite certain."

"For how long?"

She glanced at the clock on the mantelshelf. "For approximately twenty-two hours, sir," she said.

There came a pause. "Something tells me we are in the devil of a fix," he remarked, running his fingers through his hair, disordering the raven locks. "I have no remembrance of you; nor, I might add, of myself."

Adrianna had for some time been looking rather strained, but she said with admirable restraint, "Yes, I had realized that you hadn't. It is called amnesia, I believe."

"It is," he agreed. "Come here, please."

"No!" she said, becoming rigid in her chair.

He sighed again. "Rid yourself of the notion that I entertain the slightest intention of making love to you. At the moment, I'm not up to it. I only want you to prepare the sleeping draught. My head aches like all possessed."

She promptly rose and crossed to his bedside. "It will be good if you can rest," she said, measuring the laudanum and handing him the glass. "Does the doctor know you have misplaced your memory?"

His brows rose. "My recollection is none of the clearest, but I fancy he didn't say," he replied, ignoring her attempt at humor.

"He will be told. You seemed to be in perfect control of your faculties when you first regained consciousness following the accident."

"I have no memory of it. I only recall awakening this morning with the taste of laudanum in my mouth, but with no idea of who I am, nor where I am."

"Well, I can't tell you where you are, for I haven't the faintest idea, but I can tell you who you are. You, sir, are the Earl of Ravisham."

His eyelids flickered, but he said nothing.

"Ivor David John Templeton, to enumerate your names," she added. "And now, my lord, I feel for your plight, but we had better wait until you are in stouter frame to discuss the situation further."

"I suppose we should, though I will admit to a

certain curiosity. Why are you sleeping on the floor?"

To her annoyance, she flushed. "I am not sleeping on the floor," she objected, busying herself with tucking in his sheets. "My pallet is quite comfortable, thank you."

"No pallet was ever comfortable. If we are married, as you claim, what have you against my bed?"

"You are being absurd. Your head—well, you are being absurd."

"You said that twice. Flustered, are you?"

An unwilling chuckle was dragged out of her. "Your scruples are very fine, I make no doubt," she said, crossing to the door. "I am desolated to be obliged to tell you, however, that I never sleep with strangers," she added, with a smile he privately thought irresistible, before going from the room.

Chapter 3

Though no argument he could put forth had the slightest effect on Adrianna's newly acquired taste for command, still the Earl hesitated to abandon his attempt to dissuade her from her determination that they return to Twinfriars. "It is not as if I am in any wise to escort you about London," he gave as his final persuasion. "To tell you the truth, I doubt I would recognize any of my friends, should I come across them."

"I would imagine," she said, "that you were not quite hoping to go racketing about town."

"I really haven't thought about much of anything, other than my head."

"The doctor said you are to travel a short distance only. I have a strong notion you will improve rapidly once you become settled in the quiet of the country. Your friends will no doubt come to call; you should be adequately entertained."

He received with equanimity this suggestion that he could expect to forego the pleasure of her company. "Certainly," he said. "Your time will no doubt be taken up in going to London to shop."

Adrianna was momentarily startled. "Shopping!" she ejaculated and shook her head. "No. I thank you, but—no."

"You surprise me," he remarked. "I am sure your needs are not beyond my financial capabilities."

"The thing is," she said, confidingly, "I have no idea what they are."

"My resources? I assure you they are ample."

"No, silly. My needs. I have never been much in the way of shopping. I wouldn't know how to go about it."

"Nevertheless," he said, eyeing the traveling costume she had worn continuously since their marriage, "you will oblige me in this. The thought of seeing you every day in that same gown quite unnerves me."

She was forced to smile. "Not as much as it unnerves me, sir," she said. "Very well. Since it pleases you, I will purchase a few things."

"You will purchase a wardrobe consistent with your position in the world of fashion. I have in mind a lady who will, for a fee, undertake the task of dressing you. When Will returns to town, I will send word to her."

"Oh?" she said, nervously biting her lip. "Who is she?"

He knit his brow. "I don't seem to recall names and places, or recent events, though my memory seems clear in other respects. Well, never mind. I do know I can easily afford you carte blanche."

"It seems almost—almost wicked to fritter away more than modest sums of money. What if you should one day have need of it?"

"You have not so far displayed much interest in my circumstances, but I assure you I am generally accounted to be quite wealthy. Inquire of my banker if you doubt I am able to provide for you. He will inform you that the whole of my fortune is positively indecent."

She looked at him suspiciously. "It sounds like a hum to me," she said, somewhat shortly.

The Earl, after pondering this in silence for a moment, said, "I was under the impression your cousin had informed you."

"No, but—forgive me—it seems scarcely possible that you could be as rich as that!"

He stared at her. "Are you saying that you married me without knowing?" he demanded, thunderstruck.

"You number the wrong sort of females among your acquaintance," she replied, unresentful of his incredulity. "Not all of us are mercenary."

He regarded her with a lurking smile. "I thought I had nothing more to learn of your sex. I was wrong."

"Are you saying that I am—well, different from other ladies?"

"I am saying that, in my experience, you are unique."

"Oh!" she said. "Then you will have high hopes that I will behave in an exemplary way."

"I sincerely trust," he remarked, amused, "that my confidence will not prove to be misplaced. Now run along. I have a very earnest desire to quit myself of this bed."

"You will take care in coming downstairs, will you not? The steps are quite steep."

"I am not in my dotage," he replied, tossing back the covers. "You may watch me dress if you wish," he added, then chuckled to see her scurry from the room.

When he descended the stairs some hour later, his man, Upton, who thought him incapable of dressing himself, would have been much surprised. No crease marred the coat which fitted his figure exactly; his cravat was arranged to a nicety; his hair, which had a marked tendency to curl, was carefully brushed into its usual windswept style. As he stepped into the common room, he was astonished to discover Adrianna in conversation with a stranger. His jaw set. "Your mistake, sir, lies in your lamentable habit of accosting ladies to whom you have not been introduced," he said in his most blighting tones.

His quarry turned round in surprise. He was a barrel-chested man, with long arms, a short neck, and rather extravagant taste in dress. Garish, in fact. He said, somewhat too loudly, "The name is Grimcoe, my lord. I am, or was, a friend of your late Uncle William's."

The Earl raised his quizzing-glass. "That does

not come as a surprise," he said, shuddering slightly as his gaze traveled slowly over a flowered waistcoat of glorious hue and came to rest upon a carelessly tied cravat.

Grimcoe, accustomed to being snubbed, had developed a thick skin. "I was just telling her ladyship here that many's the time I've visited Twinfriars," he said jovially.

The quizzing-glass was lowered. "I trust," the Earl said, "that you will entertain no notion of doing so in future."

Grimcoe was short on wit, but long on gall. He gave a rather shaky laugh. "Your lordship would not be one to turn away an old family friend," he said with a fine show of bluff heartiness.

"You mistake, sir," the Earl replied, a faint, sweet smile curling his lips. "I am much afraid that I would."

Grimcoe blinked at him. His lordship would, he guessed, peel remarkably well. Not wishing to come afoul of a handy bunch of fives, he eased himself toward the door. "Well, now. I got business elsewhere," he said, anxious to be gone.

"I am sure you do," the Earl agreed.

Grimcoe's gaze shifted to Adrianna's face. "I daresay you're bound for London, my lady?" he inquired in hopeful accents.

Adrianna read the message in the Earl's eyes. "Why, yes, we are," she replied with a fine disregard for the truth.

"Then I'll probably see you there," Grimcoe beamed.

The Earl's hand again sought his quizzing-glass.

"I doubt it," he remarked, eyeing Grimcoe's florid countenance with distaste. "But in case we do, let me remind you I do not number my late uncle's friends among my own."

Grimcoe shot him a look of venomous dislike. "Drat if ever I did meet such a wispy buck as you," he said and departed on the words, calling to the landlord to have his horse brought out front.

Adrianna watched him go, astonished. "I have never seen you so haughty," she said, turning to face the Earl. "He was only being friendly."

"My dear, I wish you will rid yourself of the notion that all strangers can be accepted at face value."

"But if he enjoyed the esteem of your uncle—"

"Uncle William may have been a shocking loose-screw, but that waistcoat would have offended even his sensibilities. You are entirely too trusting."

"I am not! Pray, do not be so provoking! Why did you wish him to think we are off to London?"

"Would it please you to have him appear at Twinfriars? No, of course it wouldn't."

"I shouldn't think he would murder us in our beds."

"No, nothing so exciting. He would more probably attempt to—I believe the word is snaffle—whatever bauble happened to be lying about."

"Oh!" she said, digesting this. "Well, I am glad you sent him packing. I can't say I liked him very much. What are we going to do now?"

"We are going to eat our breakfast," he replied, leading her to the table.

"I don't wish to sound like a bossy female," she began, unfolding her napkin, "but I should send to London for foodstuffs, if I were you. That ham you are about to serve bears little resemblance to the one we saw at Twinfriars."

"Only too true," he remarked. "We will purchase our own supplies in the local shops."

"I presume you do not customarily carry large sums about your person?" she said, accepting her plate from his hand.

"Not enormous sums, no."

"I don't mean to infer rude things about your Uncle William, but I doubt he enjoyed any credit at all with the tradesmen."

The Earl acknowledged this home truth with a smile. "I am not my Uncle William," he pointed out.

"To the people in these parts, you're the same as," she countered, picking up her knife and fork.

"In that case, we have no choice in the matter. We will return to London."

"No!" she said, not mincing matters.

"I think," he reflected softly, "that you are become too big for your—"

"—breeches?"

"I was going to say skirts."

"You think I am being disagreeable, but the doctor was most explicit. You are concussed, and not to overdo. Leave the matter in my hands, please. I am aware Twinfriars has been shockingly neglected—"

"Shockingly neglected! It bids fair to falling down!"

"It only wants a thorough cleaning. That must be my first object; once the dust and cobwebs have been cleared away, the prospect should appear less grim."

"I was not implying you won't put forth every effort to set the house to rights. Well, it seems we are committed to Twinfriars."

"I daresay the prospect may seem dull to you, but it is otherwise with me. Before we were married, I was always made to feel beholden under someone else's roof. You cannot conceive how I am looking forward to a home of my own."

He was silent for a moment; then he smiled, and she was reassured. "I have only one request to make," he said. "The Chitterings—I really cannot abide the thought of having him around."

She was obliged to laugh. "You put me forcibly in mind of my own sentiments," she replied affably. "I took the liberty of sending for your London staff."

"Good God!" he ejaculated. "They will take to their heels at their first glimpse of the place."

"No such thing!" she objected. "Just consider the possibility of coming upon a specter in the halls. The London house will seem tame by comparison."

"They may not see it quite like that."

"Is there no romance in your soul? Anyone with the least sensibility must anticipate making the acquaintance of a ghost."

His astonishment was plain to see. "You cannot be serious!" he said, dumbfounded.

"Coachman engaged the services of several

women from the village to assist Mrs. Chittering," she replied, chuckling. "By now they should have rendered the house quite habitable."

"It would take an army!" he protested.

"I hired an army. I make no doubt the villagers think that Croesus is come amongst them."

"Doing it a bit brown, aren't you? Not five minutes past, you were reading me a lecture on our credit in the town."

"*Your* credit, sir," she said archly. "Mine is quite another matter. Coachman had only to noise it about that I am a relation of royalty."

"You never!" he gasped, stunned.

"Really, you must rid yourself of this habit you have acquired of faulting what I say with every other breath. I am related to a royal family."

"Adrianna!" he admonished, neither of them aware that he had, in the heat of the moment, employed her Christian name.

"It is very uncivil of you to doubt me," she told him roundly. "I just didn't say which royal family."

"You will forgive me for being a trifle alarmed," he replied, rising to move around behind her chair.

She gave a gurgle. "I am descended from Emperor Conrad the Second of Germany, my lord. In case you have forgotten your history, he was an eleventh-century ruler from the Palatinate. Oh, are we off to Twinfriars now?"

"We are," he replied, assisting her to her feet. "What particular lie are you planning next?"

"Well," she mused thoughtfully, "if you don't

quite like the royalty ploy, I could always say my father is a nabob."

"I think I prefer you as a princess."

"I must say I think it was a capital idea. At least we eat."

"You need have no fears on that score," he said. "My dear, the mere mention of my name is enough to insure credit anywhere in the land. Do rid yourself of the notion that you are poor."

She was immediately on the defensive. "You must think me inexperienced," she murmured, pouting slightly.

The corner of his lips twitched. "Believe me, I would never suggest such a thing," he replied with perfect gravity.

She studied him and seemed satisfied. "I think we had better go now. The coach will be out front, with perhaps the horses on the fret."

The smile lingered in his eyes; if he took exception to instruction in the care of his team, he hid it well.

To her astonishment a phaeton-and-four stood waiting before the inn. "I may know little of whipsters, but I know fiery horses when I see them," she remarked, running her eyes over the magnificently matched bays. "Do you think this wise?"

"Certainly," he replied, placing a hand beneath her elbow and leading her forward. "I am not crippled, merely addled."

Their eyes met, hers faintly doubtful, his definitely smiling. She had always despised her height, but she had to tilt her head to look up into his face. "Are you perfectly sure you won't land us in a ditch?" she inquired, allowing him to hand her to the seat.

"I haven't so far given you cause to think I will," he replied, mounting to the box beside her.

"No, but then you haven't so far driven me about," she reminded him.

He turned his head to stare at her. "Unless I am much mistaken, you disapprove of me," he remarked, gathering up the reins.

"Nonsense," she protested. "Why should I?"

"Alas, my fatal addiction to 'pugilism, curricle-racing, and gambling,' I fear."

"Odious!" she said, aware of a strong attraction. The thought that she might have come to view her handsome bridegroom with something more than a passing interest flashed through her mind, causing her to blush.

"Relax and enjoy the drive," he instructed, setting the bays forward. "This country is not of any great moment, but perhaps it won't prove boring."

"Yes, indeed," she responded, rising to the occasion. "I expect some of it must be quite pretty. When you are recovered from your injury, I imagine we could explore."

"That would be delightful," he replied, with the courtesy for which he was renowned. "I will be obliged if you will ride with me. Remember to include several habits in your wardrobe."

The reminder of the circumstances under which she came to him threw her into confusion. "Thank you, I—I believe not," she murmured, with less than her usual color.

"That's a set-down!" he remarked, turning his head to glance at her. "You do disapprove of me! I wish you will tell me what I've done to earn it."

"But you haven't—you must know I don't—I shouldn't think you could possibly believe—" Mortified, she ground to a halt, vexed with herself for being gauche.

"Are you trying to tell me that you don't ride?" he asked, smiling encouragement.

She looked quickly at him, and away. "I had naturally supposed you knew that poor relations remain discreetly in the background. Of course I don't ride."

"Then it will be my pleasure to teach you. I trust you are not afraid of horses?"

"No. Why should I be?"

"Some girls are. They claim they toss their heads and twitch."

This proved too much for her lively sense of humor. Going off on a peal of laughter, she said, "It remains only for you to discover that I have never handled the ribbons, and you will have come by your just deserts."

This ingenious bit of information caused his lips to quiver. "Not a bit of it," he chuckled. "I won't promise to turn you into an accomplished whip, but I will contrive to teach you to drive yourself about very prettily."

Her eyes grew round. "I am much obliged for the offer," she said, "but at my age, it's a little late to learn."

He looked down at her, his gray eyes twinkling. "Quite in your dotage, are you?" he said.

"Oh, no," she hastened to demur, then added honestly, "But I am five-and-twenty, sir."

"Yes, so the marriage contract states. I will say this for you: you wear your years very well."

She gave her infectious chuckle again. "It may not seem so old to you, but I must warn you, I am become set in my ways."

"The usual problem with spinsters, I take it?"

"As with aging bachelors," she agreed.

At that a laugh escaped him. "I am beginning to think it is a lucky thing I married you. What other chance could there be for a graybeard of two-and-thirty?"

"It makes it very awkward for us, but I suppose we will contrive. I have it on excellent authority that people who marry late in life get along tolerably well together."

"Good God!" he uttered blankly. "Your cousin?"

"My cousin's wife, sir."

"Lady Brandywood is something of a fool. You will find me attentive to your comfort, but I'll not play the aging Apollo to your youthful Cassandra."

"Then you won't decree that you shan't believe my prophecies?"

"Not unless you anger me."

"All is not at an end," she observed, enjoying their banter. "Don't think me such a ninny that I would be torn between the hope that you will, and dread that you won't."

"Perhaps," he said, smiling faintly, "I had better not make my credit too high with you. What would you suggest? That I give you to understand that I redress grievances with a fine show of temper?"

"Well, as to that, I am very sure that you do. However else could you have taken the thought into your head?"

He laughed. "And I was bent on doing the pretty," he said. "But alas. You cannot behave with propriety."

Chapter 4

They had by this time reached the gateposts of Twinfriars and turned onto the neglected drive. The Earl drew his team to a halt and surveyed the scene before him. "It's a dashed thicket," he observed, eyeing the overgrown shrubbery crowding the carriage way.

"Oh, I don't know," Adrianna demurred. "I think it is rather picturesque."

"Yes, I will allow that it is. I will even concede it has a certain—earthy charm."

"In that case, turning a gardener loose with pruning shears will not be your object."

He gave his horses the office to proceed. "You will become chilled if we tarry," he remarked, looking rather searchingly at her.

"Altering the trend of the conversation, are you?" she said, cutting her eyes at him.

"Just stalling for time," he replied. "I am sorry if you don't quite like it, but if I am to enhance its value, the place must be put in order."

"Undoubtedly it must," she agreed, with unimpaired composure.

"Indeed?" he said. "A moment ago you were waxing poetic over shrubbery sadly in need of trimming."

If she smiled it was so slightly that he was unaware of it. "I can think of nothing more depressing than owning a witch's haven," she said.

"That is perhaps a pity," he remarked. "You do own it."

At first she did not take in what he said. Then she did, and stared. "I don't pretend to know what you are talking about!" she gasped.

"Foolish beyond permission!" he teased. "The property is my wedding present to you."

"Of the absurdities of the world, that has to be—"

He looked faintly reproving. "I must tell you, my dear, that this habit you have fallen into of expressing yourself with the utmost disregard for ladylike reticence is vastly unbecoming. Besides, it was a surprise."

"You mean we stopped here first before going on to your family seat because—?"

"Precisely."

"Then that is why—Oh! This is terrible! You were intending to tell me, but you couldn't. Not after all I found to do was to complain! You must have thought me the most ungrateful wretch alive, let alone being horribly embarrassed to find the property in such sad case."

"Uncle William could never abide family pretentions, as he chose to term it. Said he could not see the least need for display. It is a great deal too bad he could not see the need for repairs."

"Well, he didn't. But I have a great dependence on our ability to correct his omissions."

" 'Our,' my lady?" he said. "Instead of worrying your pretty head over it, why don't you go to London shopping? You can send back fabrics and wallpapers, if you must."

"Nothing will prevail upon me to leave decisions up to workmen. Paper must be hung on the walls just so, and everyone knows patterns must be used with care. To be honest with you, I should think it sadly flat to walk into the house and find myself with nothing to do."

"Since it will give you pleasure, I withdraw my offer. In fact, I will accompany you to London."

"When you have settled it with your doctor, yes, I would enjoy that."

The Earl allowed this remark to pass, the phaeton having arrived before the house. Adrianna allowed him to lift her down, and stood critically assessing the progress made by Mrs. Chittering and her helpers. The front steps had been swept, loose shutters fastened down, and the windows polished until they shone. It would never be a building proclaimed by architects, she knew, but its mellow brickwork lent a certain charm.

"Once the lawn is mowed and the gardens tended, it won't be half bad," the Earl remarked at her elbow. "I presume my man of business referred to its size when he spoke of it as a handsome property."

"Ivy will tend to camouflage its faults," she remarked, surveying the bewildering profusion of hips and valleys comprising the roofs. "At least it will then seem all of a piece."

"Apparently past generations enlarged the structure much as their fancies dictated. Well, we have perhaps seen the worst of it. Let us go in."

The door was opened by a young girl from the village with a mop-cap on her head and a dust pan in her hand. She bobbed a curtsy, flushed to the roots of her hair, and fled. "I trust we will not have a like effect upon everyone in this neighborhood," the Earl remarked at his driest.

"She was flustered to find the hall invaded by an elegant gentleman in a coat with no fewer than—dear me, I do believe I count sixteen shoulder-capes."

The expression of annoyance on his face became even more pronounced. "Far be it from me to destroy your illusions, but I feel I should inform you that the fault lies with your bonnet," he said, laying his curly-brimmed beaver hat down upon a table.

"Much you know!" she asserted, chuckling. "It is the high crack of fashion. I scrimped for months to buy it."

The Earl looked down into her upturned face and sensed the pleading behind her smile. "You would wish me to believe our mode of dress explains the very odd reception we received," he said, smiling in return.

"We may as well conduct ourselves in a civil way. No good result can be obtained by offending the notions of the villagers who come here to work."

"I suppose you may be right. Twinfriars is too isolated for these people to find us other than a curiosity. Your presence will no doubt divert them more than mine," he added, with a disarming twinkle in his eyes.

He was interrupted in this unchivalrous assault upon her sense of the ridiculous by the appearance of Mrs. Chittering. "Well, now," she said, beaming. " 'Tis glad we are to have you back, my lord. I'm thinking you will find the late Master's rooms comfortable. We readied them up for you and her ladyship, seeing as how they're the best in the house."

"They will do, I'm sure. If you will be so kind?"

" 'Tis the first door at the top of the stairs, my lord."

"Have our baggage brought in, please, and send tea up to us. A light repast will suffice."

Mrs. Chittering dropped a curtsy and bustled away, disappointed at not learning the reason for their return. The Earl, meanwhile, tossed his driving coat across a chair and led Adrianna across the hall and up the oak staircase to the main chambers above. The sitting room was large and lofty, wainscoted with oak, hung with crimson brocade, and furnished with a profusion of sofas and chairs worthy of a palace. Adrianna paused upon the threshold, dazzled momentarily by so much magnificence. "Perhaps your Uncle William suffered from an abiding dislike of spending money for any purpose other than his own comfort," she remarked, looking around.

"Don't fall into the error of thinking him warm. I know for a fact he had fallen on evil days. He hadn't a sou."

"Had he not!" she exclaimed, her gaze coming to rest upon a painting hanging above the mantelshelf. "I do not claim to be an authority, but surely that's a Rubens!"

The Earl's hand sought his quizzing-glass, and raised it. A somber frown came upon his brow, and his mouth became grim. "It is!" he said abruptly.

The silence that followed was broken by the sound of a burned-out log expiring among its fellows in the fire. Adrianna crossed to a door standing ajar and entered the adjoining room. Three steps up on a dais stood a vast four-poster bed, hung with crimson brocade bed-curtains and piled high with down-filled pillows. "Exotic, isn't it?" the Earl remarked, a slight sardonic smile curling his lips.

Adrianna became absorbed in a minute inspection of the furnishings. "A Canaletto, two Van Dycks, a Murillo, and a Veronese," she said. "The possessions of a pauper, sir?"

The Earl returned the questioning look in her eyes with one of acute denial. "It is the first I have known of it," he said, frowning.

"The contents of this room are worth a fortune."

"So I see."

"Those cabinets are cram-full of jade and ivory."

"Yes."

"Not to mention Sevres and Meissen."

"You mentioned them," he said. "I didn't."

"Why not?" she asked, staring at him perplexed.

"Because I did not wish to," he told her frankly. "From what I understood, Uncle William was usually one step ahead of his creditors. It is confoundedly awkward to learn we have inherited more than a run-down property, but I don't see what we can do about it."

"The long and short of it is, you and your uncle did not like each other very much. Why did he make you his heir?"

"There was no one else. He should have remarried after Great-aunt Ethelroy's death, but he was never known to please anyone but himself."

"He must have loved her very much."

"No, they had barely spoken to each other for

at least twenty years. He disliked women, said they played him false, though I have an idea it was the other way around."

"I take it that, had he remarried, he would likely have made some poor female miserable."

"Yes, that is quite true," the Earl agreed.

"So you repaid him for burdening you with an unsought inheritance by thrusting it off on me. Or would just any female have suited your purpose equally as well?"

He saw the amusement in her eyes and chuckled. "Uncle William must be turning in his grave to have it come into the hands of any female at all. Well, it serves him right. He was a miserable pinch-penny where Aunt Ethelroy was concerned. You must forgive me if I perhaps appear to you to be lacking in sensibility, but it is my intention to turn Twinfriars into a property you will be proud to own."

"Yes, and I am grateful, but I must tell you that you are not at all the sort of man I first thought you were. My situation before our marriage was awkward indeed, but now I am a woman of substance no one will dare to snub me."

"Dare to do what?" he demanded, in a tone that made her jump.

"Well, in my cousin's home I was forever being asked to perform some little task generally allotted to an under-housemaid. Good God! What's that?" she gasped as the sound of a brass gong reverberated throughout the house.

"Dinner, I should imagine," he replied, giving her a thoughtful look. "Shall we go down?"

"Chittering's notions may be perfectly understandable in a stable-hand," she said, placing her hand on the arm he held out to her, "but do tell him not to startle us in that way again."

As it turned out, the would-be butler was nowhere to be seen, and since Mrs. Chittering was busy in the kitchen, they were served by a young girl from the village who simply set the dishes on the table and disappeared. The situation struck the Earl as being fantastic, but Adrianna, remarking that the morrow should see the arrival of his own servants, enjoyed a hearty meal. At last finished, she laid down her knife and fork and said, "It would be absurd for either of us to lay claim to a passion we do not feel."

The Earl, startled, choked on his wine.

"I understand that unions such as ours often prosper," she continued, pursuing her decision with relentless determination. "But I must tell you that I much prefer not to—rush things. No, you needn't show your teeth. You know perfectly well what I mean."

He hesitated and then said bluntly, "It must have been a muscle spasm. I'm not smiling."

"No, I see you aren't. For myself, I find it difficult to believe that we are married."

"It is a matter of record," he replied, at his grimmest.

"I hope this does not put you in a very dangerous humor," she murmured, unable to meet his eyes.

"You are, in fact, hoping to find me complaisant."

She was spared the necessity of answering by the entrance of Chittering. "Will yer lordship be wantin' anything more?" he asked, unceremoniously stacking the dishes upon a tray.

The Earl toyed with his quizzing-glass. "It is a source of wonderment to me how you persuaded my late uncle to keep you around. Her ladyship is retiring now. See to it a fire is kindled in her hearth."

Chittering nodded and dumped the silver on the tray before going from the room, an action which provoked the Earl to say, "Tomorrow he goes. I will pension him off."

"Yes, but it is too bad. Mrs. Chittering tries so hard."

"I will put a cottage on the estate at their disposal. It will be possible for her to remain, if you wish it."

"I do. Her loyalty will be all to me."

His brows rose. "You seem to think you have some need for her that will work to your advantage," he remarked, glancing at her in some surprise.

"No, no, nothing of the sort," she replied, laying down her napkin. "I have nothing in the world to fear, I know."

The Earl rose and moved around behind her seat. "Not from me, it seems," he said, pulling back her chair.

She flushed. "I did not mean to imply I fear you," she said, the breath catching in her throat.

"Dread is perhaps the correct term," he remarked, crossing to the door.

Chapter 5

The Earl escorted Adrianna upstairs to their sitting room, where a fire burned merrily upon the hearth. "I will leave you now," he said, opening the door. "You will be perfectly safe."

Holding out her hand, she murmured with a marked lack of composure, "Thank you. I am sensible of your—your kindness—"

"I thought you would say that," he remarked, taking her hand in his. "I see now there is a grain of truth in Uncle William's strictures."

"You mean that females are most unpredictable?"

"Most!" he agreed.

"Even maddeningly so."

"I think we might say that."

"Well, you are very obliging, but I will still bid you goodnight."

"I know. Believe me, I know."

He was gone on the words, leaving her feeling strangely bereft. Unable to compose her spirits, she wandered aimlessly around the room, fetching up before a bookcase. The volumes ranged over a wide variety of subjects, though the majority of them were concerned with art. Interested, she withdrew a book and settled down in a chair drawn up before the fire. It had been her intention to while away an hour or so before retiring, but she read on, heedless of the time, until the guttering of a candle claimed her notice. A glance at the mantel clock revealed the hour to be quite late. Feeling exhausted suddenly, she restored the volume to the bookshelf and went into the other room. Her solitary bed never seemed so lonely. For a moment she felt extremely discomfited. However strange it all might be, she was glad enough to crawl between the sheets.

Some slight noise awakened her close upon the dawn. She lay rigid, listening intently, but when no further sound reached her ears, she recollected that old structures were wont to creak, and closed her eyes again, chiding herself for suffering from an excess of sensibility. Only a very few minutes had elapsed, however, when the clank of one object striking against another jerked her wide awake. For a moment she was frightened; then, supposing the Earl had come into their sitting room, she quietly donned her negligee and picked up a candlestick still burning on the bedside table. A few steps took her to the door. She opened it and crossed the threshold, only to be brought up short by the sight of Mr. Grimcoe lifting the

Rubens down from its place above the mantel.

Her gasp of shock brought his head around; he fairly goggled, as aghast as she. "What are you doing here?" she demanded, her heart in her throat.

His astonishment lasted only a moment. "Forgive the intrusion, my lady," he begged, quickly recovering. "I had thought you were in London."

"That does not signify. Chittering should never have admitted you at—" she paused and glanced at the clock "—Good God! It is four o'clock in the morning!"

"I saw no need to disturb Chittering," he replied with a smoothness born of practice. "His late lordship suffered from the gout. I often bore him company during the long hours of the night."

"You may have been on terms while he lived, but that does not explain your walking in here unannounced."

"I had not expected to remain in the neighborhood overnight, and when I found I must, I hadn't a place to stay. It never occurred to me that the hospitality for which Twinfriars is renowned had been withdrawn."

It was a pretty enough speech, but Adrianna much doubted that Twinfriars was known for its hospitality. "You must lodge any complaint you harbor with the Earl," she said as coolly as she might.

"Oh, no, no, my lady!" he hastened to deny. "It is not my place to complain. I am very much shocked to have invaded your privacy. If you will excuse me—"

"Not so fast!" she interrupted. "I do not understand how you gained entrance into the house."

"I was not wishful of disturbing the servants, my lady. I would not deny the good Chittering his night's repose. But I have not seen his lordship. Perhaps the Earl is in London?"

"He is just a—a short distance away."

There came a silence which neither of them cared to break, Grimcoe because the slight catch in her voice had not escaped his notice, Adrianna because she did not have the least idea of the whereabouts of the Earl. Finally she broke it, saying in a voice which strove for calm, "And what, if you please, are you doing with the picture?"

He became aware he still held the Rubens in his hands, and searched his mind, fully conscious of the need for an explanation. "It was crooked," he offered, after some slight hesitation.

"Crooked!" she ejaculated blankly.

"I was straightening it," he explained quickly.

"By taking it down from the wall?" she demanded in disbelieving tones, her surprise overcoming the fear.

He pulled himself together. "I thought it best to check the wire. Your ladyship can appreciate the damage that can result when a painting crashes to the floor. It was merely that I wished to save the canvas from harm. Alas, I fear I frightened you."

"You are extremely obliging, but you will need to do better than that. In short, sir, I do not want for sense."

"I did not mean to imply that that was my reason for visiting Twinfriars."

"Then you will not object to my ringing for Chittering to show you out."

"That won't be necessary," he demurred, sidling toward the door. "I know my way."

"I would not dream of allowing you to wander over a darkened house," she insisted, crossing to the bell-pull. "You might just stumble over a painting lying forgotten on the floor."

He acknowledged her home hit with a bow, but refrained from comment, other than to renew his apologies for the intrusion. As for Adrianna, she could not relish being alone with him, but there was nothing she could do but wait. Chittering seemed to be taking an unconscionable time in answering her summons; when he did appear, her feeling of unease gave way to one of great insecurity. Chittering took silent but obvious exception to Grimcoe's presence in the house, as he should have done. For her peace of mind, she followed them to the head of the stairs to witness Grimcoe's departure. It was not until she saw Chittering close and bolt the front door after him that she returned to her rooms and turned the key in the lock of her own door.

When she told the Earl of it at the breakfast table the following morning, he took her to task. "You should have roused me!" he said, staring at her aghast. "I would have gotten to the bottom of the matter very speedily."

She looked guilty. "Grimcoe was as shaken as I," she assured him.

"He was up to no good. Uncle William endured a great deal of pain during his final illness. He could not bear to have anyone around. Whatever Grimcoe was after, the old boy knew nothing of it."

"I wish I knew how he gained entrance here. When Chittering let him out, he had to unlock the door. It was bolted from the inside."

"Are you certain?"

"Grimcoe said he came in by the terrace door, but Mrs. Chittering says it had been nailed shut for the past year. The lock is broken."

"Many old houses have a secret passage. We will discover if this one has. I cannot fancy strangers coming and going at will without our knowing of it."

She looked thoughtful. "Grimcoe came for the Rubens. I am sure of it."

"No. A lesser painting, perhaps, but the Rubens? I think not. What use would it be to him? He could not expect to sell it; no one would purchase a masterpiece from a man whose possession of it must be brought in question."

"Well, there was never anything like it, I'm sure. To think that I should wake to find a criminal in the room! I was never so shocked in my life!"

"It was certainly unexpected, but that does not explain why you failed to send for me."

"I could recite you a score of reasons, but one will suffice. I hadn't any notion where to find you. But this is far from the purpose, sir. Please ring for Chittering. If there is a secret passage, he may know of it."

It appeared that he didn't. When he answered the summons, it was evident he was much affected by the events of the night before and was hard put to keep his hands from shaking. The Earl soon dismissed him, only waiting until they were alone to say, "Grimcoe is not in this thing by himself, whatever it may be. I need hardly tell you that searching for a secret way into the house could turn out to be a bore."

"You mean it could prove a dusty, dirty chore."

"It will be a chore, yes. Please do not add to it by asking to join in."

"Shall you show it to me when you find it?"

"By no means," he replied. "You won't be here to see it. The opening will be found and sealed."

She looked thoughtful. "I wonder what Grimcoe will do next?" she mused, sipping her coffee.

"Yes, I can see you do. He will return to London, unless I miss my guess."

"Empty-handed? I find that hard to believe."

"If my suspicions are correct, he can be no more than a go-between."

"Between whom?"

"I wish I knew. Someone of far more intelligence than he possesses, I should think."

"What do you intend to do?"

"Wait upon events."

"Upon his next move, you mean. Or rather, upon his orders from the person who hired him."

"Something of the sort, yes. But that is nothing to the point either. The fact that it is known that Twinfriars houses paintings of value precludes our leaving them here. I need hardly tell you that we leave for London shortly."

She was shaken, but after a moment agreed enough to say, "I should agree that Chittering is insufficient protection against theft."

"Certainly not. But theft of what? Not the paintings themselves, assuredly. And not by Grimcoe either. If I am correct, someone behind the scene who dares not expose himself pulls the strings."

"This is marvelous indeed!" she exclaimed. "Do make up your mind. Is it the paintings, or isn't it?"

"Shall I be frank with you?"

"Quite frank, sir!"

"I haven't a clue."

She gazed at a point just beyond his shoulder. "The fact that you haven't may mean you have," she said somewhat vaguely. "Very well. We return to London. But the phaeton will be crowded, mind."

"You ride in Uncle William's coach with the art, my dear. I go in the phaeton."

"I see now that there is a great deal in what the doctor says! The blow to your head disordered your intellect!"

"You still go in the coach."

"You are abominable, sir! Selfish, self-centered, and thoroughly disagreeable! And besides, you are concussed."

"Yes, I am, am I not?" he replied, at his driest. "I am afraid I was forgetting that."

Chapter 6

Adrianna's arrival in Grosvenor Square was witnessed by Lady Palmer from the windows of Lady Temple's first-floor withdrawing room. The appearance of a somewhat seedy coach did not occasion more than a fleeting glance, until it drew to a halt before the door of Ravisham House. "Merciful heavens!" she exclaimed, craning her neck. "It's Ivor's chit!"

Lady Temple put aside her embroidery frame and joined her visitor at the bay. By this time Chittering had climbed down from the box and opened the coach door. "He will need nerves of iron," she remarked, observing Adrianna's progress up the steps. "It would appear our fair bride is more interested in art than clothes."

Lady Palmer's initial surprise gave way to a very cynical amusement. "I told Ivor that marriage would be his undoing," she said in a slightly unsteady voice.

It was an unwise remark, for it gave Lady Temple an opportunity to say it was a pity that the most unexceptional girls so often procured a husband. To do her justice, she spoke without malice. After all, Lila was a widow. If she chose to carry on an affair with Ravisham, no one threw up their hands in horror, so long as they were discreet.

It did not need her friend's words to harden the look in Lady Palmer's eyes, though the crushing rejoiner did put her slightly out of countenance. "Confess it affords you no little amusement," she said somewhat snidely.

Lady Temple smiled. "Why should it?" she said. "I was never in your confidence. Did you think to get Ravisham?"

Lady Palmer became jarred out of the temporary dismals. "Lord, what a bee you are, once you take an idea under your bonnet. Of course I didn't think it. Ivor would never marry a widow, you know he wouldn't. Not that I wished it," she hastened to add. "He is excessively proud, and so am I!"

But she had wished it. And the worst of it was, he knew it, had known from the beginning. He was extremely obliging, but the subject of marriage had needed only to arise for him to withdraw into a shell. Worse, the steel under his polite demeanor hinted at alienation, should she persist.

A sudden exclamation from Lady Temple interrupted her thoughts. "Here is Ravisham now," she said, twitching the curtains aside the better to see. "I will say he drives to an inch. Those bays of his look hard to handle—and I do know something about horses."

Lady Palmer withdrew a slight bit from view. "Do not let him see us staring, I implore you!" she begged. "He will think me crass!"

Lady Temple raised her brows, her momentary anger giving way to amusement. Ravisham had married for an heir; for all his premarital philandering, he would remain loyal to his wife. Lila might as well resign herself to the inevitable.

The subject of all this attention bounded up the front steps of Ravisham House with the exuberance of a boy. Lady Palmer had flattered herself that she knew him, but she would not have considered for a moment that he could be rushing to share his joy with Adrianna. He knew just what he would say. What he did say, the instant he put his head around her door, was, "I am sure you are too much the hoyden to be the wife of any gentleman."

Adrianna gasped and reached for her negligee. "I was only amusing myself," she said with unwonted stringency.

"By dancing around in your chemise?"

"You cannot have remembered to knock. One customarily does, you know."

"And I thought a husband enjoyed certain prerogatives!"

"If you wish to know what I think," she said, "you are very well pleased with yourself."

He bowed. "You perceive before you a man of great reliability," he said. "Is that not so?"

A slight smile curved her lips. "Upon occasion, amazingly so," she agreed.

"I need not have mentioned it," he murmured. "My lamentable memory, you know."

"Ivor!" she gasped, rushing forward to grasp his hands. "You have it back! I am so very glad! When did it happen?"

"The moment I turned into Grosvenor Square," he replied, raising her fingers to his lips. "This calls for a celebration. Where shall we go? Vauxhall Gardens?"

She looked doubtful. "I suppose we could, if you insist."

He crossed to the bell-pull. "Heaven forbid, my dear. I will have a bottle of champagne sent up."

"If you are disappointed, we will go. It will take me only a moment to—"

"Dress?" he interrupted. "No, you look charming just as you are."

A flush crept into her cheeks. She said, striving to make her tone light, "I will set about repairing the deficiencies in my wardrobe first thing in the morning. I shouldn't wish you to be ashamed of me."

"I could never be ashamed of you, Adrianna," he protested, strolling forward to seat himself upon the sofa.

She felt herself flush more rosily still. "You are being kind," she murmured, nervously twisting the gold band encircling the third finger of her left hand.

"I'm not kind," he protested, taking the hand in his and drawing her down to the seat beside him. "I am—hopeful."

She returned the clasp of his fingers, and said half-doubtfully, half-convincingly, "You must not be, my lord. At least, not for now."

"Aren't we being rather unsure of ourselves?" he murmured, smiling.

She returned the smile, but fleetingly. "You would not have it any other way," she said.

"Your notions are charming, my dear, but life would be dull indeed if we had no pleasures to anticipate," he replied and kissed her.

Adrianna emerged from the embrace slightly disconcerted. "There is something I must know," she said, withdrawing her hand from his.

"Certainly," said his lordship.

She half turned on the sofa and looked resolutely at him. "The other day I asked you why you insisted we marry without delay. I am sorry to have to say it, but you put me off."

Slightly taken aback, he reached his hand for his quizzing-glass and toyed with it. "I regret having given that impression," he murmured reassuringly.

"You said you were sorry that we could not have become better acquainted before our nuptials took place."

"Yes, I remember that I did."

"I don't know what it signifies, but I would like to have you explain it. If you don't mind, that is."

"Not at all. I was avoiding a horrible fate dreamed up for me by an aunt."

She frowned. "I daresay you are laughing at me, but I assure you I am most serious."

"I would never be rude to you, Adrianna," he objected mildly. "Such a pretty name: Adrianna."

"It's an odious name, sir. I was given it on account of a novel Mama happened to be reading when I was born. The heroine's name was Anna, you understand."

"Perfectly," nodded his lordship.

"The story took place on the shores of the Adriatic Sea."

His lips quivered. "A logical combination," he said.

"Yes," she agreed. "Mama always said that was so. For myself, I think my face is something of a Jane."

His lordship surveyed the face. "It would be a pity," he said. "Adrianna suits you."

She looked at him rather shyly. "Well, it cannot signify speaking of it," she said. "What was the horrible fate dreamed up for you by an aunt?"

"Marriage to a quiz who just happens to have a distant family connection. The trouble is, Papa's sisters, and there are five of them, are all antidotes themselves."

"I wish you will be sensible," she said, laughing. "You are making this up."

"Not at all. Wait until you meet them. Or rather, wait until you meet the eldest of them. Now there's a disagreeable old harridan for you. When she went so far as to pen an announcement of my engagement and threatened to send it to the *Gazette*, it behooved me to take action. I wouldn't have bet against the chance that she would do it."

"You are roasting me! No one would put you in such a position, even if they did think it was time you became regularly established. Your consequence would have obliged you to honor the announcement."

"I'm not so sure of that. The damsel of their choice was a lady of the highest respectability, and somewhat along in years—been an ape-leader for as long as I can remember, in fact. She is also scrawny, and—worse—she drags her hair back into a bun. Gives her an expression of perpetual surprise. Thank you, no. I prefer comfortably rounded females with red hair and unbelievable blue eyes."

"It is a good thing you refused to offer for her," she said, ignoring this last remark. "I daresay you were used only to the most ravishing of females."

"I will allow I thought so, until I saw you. My aunts, in any event, are glad I have settled down."

"I fancy they consider me an interloper."

"No, they feel confident you can be trusted to behave just as you ought. At least they have high hopes of it. Just don't become too comfortable. Aunt Flournoy will doubtless issue an invitation for you to present yourself in Cavendish Square. If you'll take my advice, you won't go."

"How could I refuse?" she asked earnestly. "I am the cause of their plans for you going astray."

"They had nothing to do with my marrying you, regardless of how it sounds. I knew how it would be the first time I saw you. I only rushed our wedding day to keep them from upsetting my own plans."

"Well, I must admit, from all you have said, that I fail to see why I was not what you expected me to be."

"I expected you to be a fortunate addition to my bed. I did not expect to fall in love with you."

She stole a glance at him from under her lashes. "You are outrageous, do you know it?" she said. "I wonder I don't take offense."

"But I haven't insulted you, my dear," he objected mildly.

She appeared to consider this reply acceptable. "Who resides in the house next door?" she asked suddenly.

"Lady Temple. But you must not let it distress you," he added, puzzled at the query.

"Another antidote?" she said, laughing.

"A very high stickler indeed, my dear—at least in public. In private, no. By means unknown to me, she has succeeded in introducing the oddest people into the highest circles."

"Carries on orgies at home, does she?"

"No. Just abysmally boring soirees."

"She sounds abhorrent."

"She is quite amiable, really. But then, with her formidable bosom, she would need to be. In any event, she has persuaded the ton that she is not just in the ordinary style."

"I wish I might meet her," she remarked, smiling.

"You will, the minute you cross the sacred threshold of Almack's. I imagine you must rank high on her list of eligible young matrons. Living next door to her has its drawbacks, but at least she won't find it necessary to be forever paying us a call. She can spy on us from her own windows without putting herself to much exertion."

"Then on no account must we quarrel on our front doorstep. I am excessively sorry that we can't, but when I arrived I did catch her peering at me from behind the curtains. I shouldn't wonder at it if an amusing anecdote doesn't shortly go the rounds. Only think how very mortifying for you that will be!"

His lips twitched, but he replied in a fairly steady voice, "I daresay she will paint a moving picture of your virtues."

"If you count a shabby coach and a wrinkled gown as virtues, yes, she will be moved. So will the smartly dressed lady who was with her. Not that I mind, but she fairly gaped. Do you know her? She was blonde and tall—quite luscious, in fact."

He flushed so slightly she would have missed it had she been less perceptive. Lightly scolding her for being guilty of peeping at the neighbors, he added, "The coach has been returned to Twin-friars, and we will see to your wardrobe tomorrow. You will dazzle the fashionable, my dear, Lady Temple notwithstanding."

He would have been shocked had he guessed how much she knew of his past, and how much she had been amused by the more repeatable of his indiscretions. She gave him a speaking glance and said, "I won't say I don't care a rush for looking my best, for I do. How I have hated my dowdiness! But no more! I intend to purchase more stylish gowns than—than anyone."

Her tongue had very nearly slipped. The lovely blonde could only be Lady Palmer, she knew, and wondered how much of that lady's wardrobe owed its existence to the purse of the noble Earl.

Chapter 7

At the end of three weeks Adrianna was at last ready to sally forth into society. The Earl had, so it was rumored, spread the ready about with a lavish hand. So much so, in fact, that not a decent thread could be found at any shop in town. It was an exaggeration, of course, but enough of a kernel of truth clung to the report to overset Lady Palmer's already overwrought constitution. The shock his marriage had occasioned had been productive of a fit of the dismals, but tales of his devotion to his wife (which she tried, without much success, to doubt) set the seal to her collapse. She took to her bed, a pale and interesting victim of a highly colorful ailment to her back, and resisted the entreaties of Lady Temple to return to the giddy round of fashionable squeezes where in the past she had been wont to be gay to the point of dissipation. This self-imposed exile lasted until she talked herself into believing that Ravisham danced attendance on his wife only to throw off gossip ruinous to her own standing in the world. These agreeable reflections were put to flight the moment she reappeared upon the social scene. Adrianna's praises were on everyone's tongue. She had, it seemed, become the ruling Toast.

The question that society longed to ask and yet dared not bring up concerned the Earl's relationship with the fair Palmer. That she was his mistress was perfectly well known; that speculating on the outcome was a waste of time immediately became apparent. He continued correctly courteous when they met in public, with no hint of his intentions appearing either in his demeanor or on his face.

But if society was prepared to let the matter rest, Lady Palmer was not. She received him in her boudoir on the afternoon of the very morning she sent round a missive begging him to call. He let himself into the house with his own key (which was not surprising since he owned the property) and strolled into her presence unannounced. "Your most obedient, my dear," he said, raising to his lips the fingers she held out to him. "You are looking particularly lovely today."

She smiled coquettishly. "I was afraid you might not notice," she remarked, leading him across the room to the chaise longue before the fire. "Shall we make ourselves comfortable?"

He watched her dispose herself in a reclining position and remarked humorously, "If you made yourself any more comfortable, my dear Lila, you would be naked."

"It is a new negligee," she said. "Do you like it?"

"Immeasurably," he replied, reflecting pensively that he would no doubt be called upon to pay for it.

"I have nothing on under it," she admitted, moving over to give him room.

"So I see," he said, sitting down beside her and running an appreciative eye over the generous curves clearly visible beneath the gauze. "I received your note at noon. It sounded urgent. How may I serve you?"

"You may kiss me," she replied, holding out her arms.

"I might, of course," he said, possessing himself of her hands. "You will perhaps recall, however, that I am married."

"I don't wish to recall it at the moment. Why did you do it, Ivor?"

He released her hands and said distantly, "I have no intention of discussing it."

"You mean it doesn't concern me, I suppose."

"I did not say so."

She felt the snub, but managed to smile. "No,

you are too polite. Does your wife know that you are here?"

He fished his snuff box from a pocket and flicked it open. "A cross-examination can be wearying, I fear," he remarked, taking a pinch between finger and thumb.

She had not meant to ask it, but the words popped out almost of their own accord. "Shall we continue on as before?" she asked and waited breathlessly for his reply.

His brows rose. "I had not supposed that you would contemplate doing so," he said. "No happy result could obtain for you from an affair with a married man."

She leaned forward and encircled his neck with her arms. "Ivor, my love," she murmured, her mouth very close to his. "I cannot help myself. I must have you."

He stared into her eyes, his smile a little wry. "I assure you, my dear, I am filled with compassion," he murmured, his thoughts veering to his own frustration at being held at bay. "But my sense of propriety prevents—"

He got no further. Her lips moved against his in little nibbling kisses, became sensuous. "Just this one last time," she begged, snuggling closer.

Removing her arms from about his neck, he said gently, "Try to understand, Lila. I would have been the last to suspect that I could become romantic, but it appears I have. You will forgive me, I trust."

She colored slightly. "Don't be absurd," she said.

81

"The mighty Earl of Ravisham in love with his wife? I don't believe it!"

"Once a rip, always a rip?" he asked, smiling ruefully.

"It is hardly in your style!"

"No, it isn't, is it?" he agreed.

"I should have supposed you to be past the age of fustian, Ivor," she remarked, a look of regret creeping into her eyes. "Well, it is a great deal too bad."

"Do not cast yourself down, my dear. You are a handsome woman. You will find some other man to—er, step into my shoes, I'm sure."

"You must know that my affairs are in a muddle—in short—"

"You need not be concerned. I apprehend it will be my privilege to see you square with the world."

"I am in rather deep, I'm afraid."

"Yes, I suspect you are," he replied, rising to seat himself at her desk before the window. "I will be obliged if you will suggest a sum."

She was too clever a woman to name a figure much above a trifling amount. Casting her a perfectly knowing glance, he withdrew his checkbook from a pocket and dipped a quill into the standish. Watching his hand move back and forth across the draft, she knew full well it would be the last check she would receive from him. He was buying her off; there was no blinking it. Feeling cheap, she flushed.

"I have made it out for five thousand," he said, shaking the sand off the paper.

"Five thousand!" she gasped, surprised. "I shouldn't have thought it would be for so much!"

"Have I ever been clutch-fisted?" he smiled, handing it to her. "You realize I will expect you to make other arrangements for your future, but you may, of course, remain for a time at this address. I will so instruct my man of business."

"How considerate you are, Ivor! I will find some way to repay your—"

"I do not ask payment."

"Yes, I know. I only wish this weren't good-bye. Perhaps you will wish to visit me from time to time. My bed is—"

"Lila, don't say it!"

"Then I shan't see you again?"

"I do not," he smiled, "envisage the possibility of our not meeting in the future. It is a small world, my dear."

She had to laugh. "If you were to display an excess of civility toward me in the presence of your wife, I make no doubt you would be ill-advised. I do not say you should cut me dead, but —well, you know what I mean."

He bowed. "Perfectly," he said.

"I have a high opinion of you, Ivor. We have dealt extremely together, you and I. It's too bad it has to end."

"Lila, there is no future in the life you have chosen to lead up till now. You do not want for sense. Marry some man who will provide for you before your youth and beauty fade."

"And whom would that be, pray?"

"Someone you could love."

"Don't be stuffy," she laughed, crossing with him to the door. "I live my life to suit myself. There is something a little shocking about it, perhaps, but you will admit it is a way to earn a living."

He gazed down at her, an inscrutable expression in his eyes. "Tell me," he said. "Have you considered me an easy touch?"

She glanced away, unable to sustain his regard. "Not at all," she faltered. "Shall I ring for the porter to show you out?"

"No, I know my way," he replied dryly and took his leave of her.

It was past four o'clock when he arrived home in Grosvenor Square. "Ah—Edward," he said, strolling into his study. "I have a matter of some delicacy for you."

"Certainly, my lord," Mr. Longworth replied, rising.

"The house in Cavendish Square. Its present tenant is a former—friend of mine. Do you know to whom I refer, Edward?"

"Yes, sir, I do."

"You are a prince among secretaries, my dear boy. I had no notion that you knew."

"Yes, sir, my lord," Mr. Longworth repeated, startled.

"Yes. Well. Where were we?" the Earl wondered. "Ah, yes. Cavendish Square. You will find out upon what date my—friend plans to vacate the premises. I am afraid it may become a bit awkward for you, but I feel sure you will contrive."

"I will do my best, sir."

"Take my advice, my dear Edward, and do not acquire a—friend for yourself. The parting can be—shall we say, a trifle demeaning?"

"I hadn't planned to, sir," Mr. Longworth replied, lips twitching.

"I need not have mentioned it," the Earl remarked. "My maladroitness, you know."

Mr. Longworth, who understood his lordship perfectly well, permitted himself a slight smile. "May I inquire if I am to institute eviction proceedings, should it become necessary?"

"Certainly not!" the Earl replied. "I have it on the best authority that I am an easy touch."

"Good God!" Mr. Longworth ejaculated, stunned.

The Earl smiled wryly. "I am much afraid He has little to do with it," he remarked and left the room.

He met Adrianna crossing the hall. She was dressed for the street in a gown of muted stripes and a hat with a number of curling plumes. "There you are, my dear," he said. "Are you coming in or going out?"

"Coming in. Really, Ivor, I can't remember when I have been so provoked! Six hundred and fifty guineas, indeed!"

"Tell me about it," he invited, holding open the door into the small salon.

"If you wish to know what I think," she said, preceding him into the room, "Madame Clotilda is a greedy fool! I make not the slightest doubt she will know better in future."

"I apprehend she has displeased you in some way."

"I should rather think she has!" she replied, looking scornful. "I never dreamed they were real!"

"I gather a gown from Madame Clotilda's establishment failed to measure up to standard."

"The bodice was sewn all over with diamonds! With diamonds, mind!"

"It is my inquisitive disposition, no doubt, but I fail to perceive your problem."

"But I have already told you!" she said impatiently. "The bill was for six hundred and fifty guineas!"

"Do not let it distress you, my dear. Edward is most efficient. You may rely on him."

"No, my allowance is already very generous, and I intend to live within it. I have returned the gown."

"I would never question any expenditure you wished to make, Adrianna. Please allow me to adequately provide for you," he said, the check to Lady Palmer very much on his mind.

She shook her head. "I am running horribly late, Ivor," she murmured, glancing at the gilt clock on the mantelshelf. "If we are to arrive at the opera on time, I should dress."

He came up to her. "I am the most fortunate of men," he remarked, taking her into his arms. "You do not look upon me as an easy mark."

"A what!" she demanded, startled.

"Never mind," he said and kissed her. "Well, run along and dress. I shouldn't wish you out of all patience with me."

The evening started out pleasantly enough, with nothing to indicate it would end in disaster. Adrianna had descended the stairs on time, a vision in turquoise lace, to take her seat at the dining table on the Earl's right hand. "Ivor, the most marvelous thing," she said, unfolding her napkin. "I met an old school chum of yours this morning in Madelaine Carnaby's boudoir."

"Her boudoir?" he repeated, much surprised.

"Well, but there's nothing in that," she replied, smiling at the butler serving the soup. "Thank you, Simpson. It has become quite the rage, Ivor. Gentlemen assist one in the selection of one's gown and make suggestions for the arrangement of one's hair."

"A custom imported from the Continent, I presume?" he asked, brows raised.

"You want to know if it is modest. It is. One doesn't admit the gentlemen until one's peignoir is on."

"Thus the matter becomes comprehensible," he remarked, with only the faintest quiver of his lips. "That is undoubtedly a comfort to the husband."

"Yes, but you see, he would never understand a lady's toilet. He is only a husband."

"That is undoubtedly a drawback," he agreed, leveling his quizzing-glass at the poached fish presented for his inspection. "Turbot, Simpson? I think not. The scalloped oysters, perhaps."

"It put me in mind of a performance I once saw in Drury Lane," she continued chattily. "The actor upon the stage simpered about in much the same way as Lord Belderbrock."

The Earl, who was in the act of serving himself from the oyster casserole, looked up quickly and said, "Do not tell me he's the 'old school chum' of whom you spoke!"

"W-well, yes," she murmured, confused by the incredulity in his tone.

"You begin to interest me profoundly," he said. "I had thought him out of the country."

"Yes, but he is back, you see. It was he who introduced the idea of gentlemen assisting a lady with her toilet."

"I thought perhaps it might be he, the moment you said he was back. May I ask what you thought of him?"

"I thought him excessively silly. His manner, I mean, not his clothing. I can't favor a neckcloth so high as to render a gentleman incapable of turning his head, but if he considers the style worth the discomfort, it is his business, not mine. What I cannot understand is his stuffing himself into garments too small for his figure, but again, it is his concern."

"Do not tell me Belderbrock has run to fat!"

"Yes, but not in the legs, you know. Lord Wood —did I mention that he was present?—Lord Wood whispered that his lordship's man fills them out by pouring sawdust into his hose. And Sir George Cremens told me he sleeps in chicken-skin gloves. I imagine he does. His hands are certainly red enough."

"Perhaps," he said dryly, "I should accompany you on your morning round of calls."

She laughed. "Well," she said, "the whole thing seems stupid to me. I shan't invite gentlemen into my boudoir."

The Earl's eyes met hers across the expanse of white linen cloth. "You comfort me," he said.

"I shouldn't care for the aroma of Circassian hair-oil smelling up my room," she added, spoiling the effect. "Ivor, promise me you won't cultivate a lisp."

He looked amused. "I hadn't contemplated doing so," he remarked, touching his napkin to his lips.

She looked seriously at him. "I find it hard to believe that Lord Belderbrock could be your friend," she said. "Is he?"

"Did he say so?" he inquired.

"Not—quite," she admitted. "But he gave that impression."

After a moment he picked up the decanter of claret and refilled his glass. "I should imagine he will be at pains to give all the world that impression," he remarked a little dryly. "I can't say I care for it."

Nor did his Aunt Flournoy care for it when she heard of it at her own dinner table at approximately the same time. She not only held every fop of the dandy-set in the utmost abhorrence, she set great store by the Earl's consequence as head of the family. Ravisham might rate himself cheap in his choice of friend, but Lady Flournoy recognized in the circumstances both a threat and a menace. Of all the throng present in the King's Theater

89

when the Earl and Countess of Ravisham arrived, his aunt, comfortably ensconced in Lady Jersey's box, was by far the most formidable.

The curtain falling on the first act provided an opportunity for her to beckon him to her side. His own box being full of friends stopping in, he shrugged and strolled away, fetching up at Lady Jersey's box some four minutes later. "I am happy to see you looking so well, Aunt," he said, bowing with exquisite grace over the hand she held out to him.

"So it's to be a glib tongue, is it?" she demanded, indicating the chair just vacated by Mr. Brummell. "Don't play the fool with me, Ravisham. What's this I hear about Belderbrock?"

"I couldn't say," he replied mildly. "You have yet to tell me what you heard."

"Don't play off your trick on me, sir. You know perfectly well what I mean. Has he become your friend?"

"Not to my knowledge."

"He's a mischief maker, boy, and an expert with a pistol. Do you wish a bullet through your heart?"

"I believe myself capable of averting that particular calamity."

"No doubt Lord Colby thought the same. Have you forgotten that Belderbrock fled the country for slaying him in a duel?"

"I understand that Belderbrock is no longer a fine figure of a man."

"He need not be, to pull a trigger."

"One does not pull a trigger. One squeezes it."

"Either way, you're just as dead."

"Nevertheless, dear Aunt, you must permit me to—er, go to perdition in my own way."

"Well, if you wish to know what I think, and I make not the smallest doubt you don't, you are foolish beyond permission!"

"Am I to call him out for laying claim to a friendship that does not exist?"

"Don't be an ass!"

The Earl seemed not the least bit moved. "If others only understood me half so well," he remarked absently, his eyes on Adrianna in their box across the way.

Lady Flournoy followed the direction of his regard. "If you had a grain of sense you would chaperone that chit," she said. "I never dreamed you would stand idly by while she took up Belderbrock. If you will take my advice, you will supervise your wife!"

"But only think how fatiguing," he murmured, and turned to pay his respects to Lady Jersey.

The subject of Lady Flournoy's concern, meanwhile, had made his way to Ravisham's box. Desiring nothing better than to promote himself with the Earl, he became quite put out to find his lordship absent. Nor was his disappointment assuaged very much by the sight of Lady Ravisham tête-à-tête with young Viscount Shirley. Adrianna, observing his expression of acute disdain, felt her hackles rise. "If you are come to see my husband," she said, "he isn't here."

Lord Belderbrock reddened. "One has no need of mortal man when in the presence of a goddess," he said, bowing with a flourish.

Adrianna, her own annoyance unassuaged, frowned. "You must not think I desire your compliments, for I don't," she said, knowing she was being rude, and not caring.

A black scowl came upon Lord Belderbrock's face. "You must learn to treasure any flattering phrases that come your way, my dear," he said. "His lordship the Earl is accustomed to more accomplished charmers than yourself at his beck and call."

Viscount Shirley, first appalled by Belderbrock's temerity in entering the Earl's box uninvited, then infuriated by the thinly veiled reference to Lady Palmer, leaped to his feet. "You blackguard!" he gritted through his teeth. "I'm calling you out for this!"

There was a moment of stunned silence, during which Lord Belderbrock stood staring at the Viscount as one unable to believe his ears. "Take care, you young hothead, before I take offense," he said at last, turning away.

Viscount Shirley reached out a hand and seized him by the arm. "Weaseling out, are you?" he said fiercely. "I took you for a coward from the outset! Which will it be? Pistols or swords?"

Lord Belderbrock bowed. "Pistols!" he said. "My seconds will wait upon yours at a convenient hour tomorrow. I presume you have friends willing to support you?"

The Viscount named Lords Cogham and Reston, and Lord Belderbrock withdrew from the box, leaving Adrianna's knight-errant free to resume his seat. The entire episode had used up less than

three minutes by the clock and had gone un-
noticed, to her very great relief. She was certainly not displeased at being championed. The
Earl, however, when she told him of it while they
were en route home, was most assuredly displeased.

Chapter 8

Somewhat before noon on the following day,
while he was still abovestairs, Lord Belderbrock's
valet informed him that the Earl of Ravisham
was below. Instructing his man to deny him, he
resumed his perusal of the morning paper, a trifle
abstracted. The sound of the valet's step descending the stairs was followed almost immediately by
the sound of the Earl's coming up them. "You surprise me, Belderbrock," he remarked, strolling into
the room. "I should think you would have expected me."

"I'm sure I don't know why you think that!"

Belderbrock snapped. "Well, say what you have come to say, but be brief."

"As you wish, my dear fellow," the Earl said, smiling mirthlessly. "Why did Viscount Shirley force a quarrel on you? You will appreciate my curiosity, I'm sure."

Belderbrock gathered his scattered wits. "As to that, I couldn't say. Young men today become violent for no reason at all."

"Shirley would not agree. I had the felicity of paying him a call on my way here. He regrets— modesty prevents me from repeating his exact words—he regrets my interest in the affair, but bows to my superior claim."

Belderbrock shot him a surly look. "The young fool took exception to a perfectly innocent remark of mine. There is no accounting for it. He must be out of his mind."

"From what he tells me, you insulted my Countess. He seemed to think that sufficient reason."

There came an uncomfortable pause. "I don't profess to understand why you are so anxious to believe him, but that's neither here nor there. I have never backed away from meeting my man, nor will I now!"

"I hate being tiresomely repetitious," the Earl drawled in silken tones, "but I must inform you that Shirley has run his race. I trust I am not wrong in thinking myself an acceptable substitute in his stead."

"I have no quarrel with you, Ravisham, if that

is what you are driving at. I have no intention of calling you out."

"Do you know, Belderbrock," the Earl replied pensively, "I will almost relish running you through. Yes, we will fight with swords. You will challenge me, I assure you."

"You cannot think that I will!"

"You will forgive me for disputing you, I'm sure. If the insult was of enough moment to precipitate Shirley into forcing a duel, you may be sure I will not ignore it. Attend me, Belderbrock! I will insult you publicly until you are forced to challenge me. Do not make the mistake of thinking I will become the aggressor. You would elect to fight with pistols. As the challenged party, I will opt for the blades."

"Insult me at your pleasure. I am indifferent to what people say."

"Every man has his Achilles heel. I will find yours, believe me. Unless you should elect to retire from the London scene."

Lord Belderbrock went cold with sudden fear. "Really, Ravisham," he gasped, shuddering. "Your manner—"

"I presume I have made my position clear," the Earl remarked and went from the room without a backward glance.

Feeling confident that he had averted a scandal, the Earl set out in the direction of his club; then, changing his mind, he returned home to Grosvenor Square. He would have gone upstairs immediately had he known that Adrianna was experiencing qualms. She had had time to think over the disastrous results of her wayward tongue. What had seemed perfectly justified the evening before was now seen as reprehensible. There was no putting it off; she may as well go downstairs and face the Earl.

His lordship, a footman informed her upon inquiry, had come in a short time before, and could be found in the bookroom. Adrianna drew a ragged breath, as though something were lodged in her throat, and went on down the hall with a step that slowed imperceptibly as she approached the library door.

The Earl was seated at his desk with his back to the room, staring into space. Adrianna paused a moment in the threshold, admiring the set of his shoulders in the close-fitting coat of blue superfine. He was evidently deep in thought, for he remained unaware of her presence until she spoke his name. Turning his head, he saw her and immediately rose. "Forgive me, my dear," he said, moving around the desk. "I was abstracted and did not hear you come in."

She became involved in sedulously inspecting her shoes. "If you don't mind, Ivor," she murmured, "I'd as lief get it over with."

"Get what over with?" he inquired, walking forward across the expanse of Aubusson carpet that separated them.

"My—my scold. I know you must be amazingly put out with me."

"Must I?" he said, a smile quivering at the corners of his mouth.

"I will own I don't blame you in the least for being angry."

"Oh?" he said, unable to withstand the temptation to tease. "Am I angry?"

Her gaze flickered from her slippers to his face and back again. "You see, he—Lord Belderbrock, I mean—irritated me."

He smiled encouragement. "I can quite understand that he would," he said.

"I didn't set out to be—to be—well, vulgar."

"I trust not, my dear."

She drew a long breath and raised her eyes again. "I know you will need to send me away until—until people have some other scandal to talk about, only I do h-hope you will have me back when they h-have!"

The veriest hint of surprise flickered across his face. "There will be no scandal," he assured her, catching her hands. "I have—er, called off the duel."

Her grasp tightened on his. "Called it off?" she repeated, uncomprehending. "But how could you? It is between Viscount Shirley and Lord Belderbrock!"

"Viscount Shirley has abrogated his role in the affair."

"But I don't understand. Viscount Shirley challenged him."

"His lordship will withdraw the challenge. You see, my love, I really could not permit the duel to come off as scheduled."

She stared at him, dumbfounded. "No, of course not," she said, from lack of anything else to say.

"I left Belderbrock no choice in the matter," he explained, smiling into her eyes. "I flatter myself that I handled him rather well."

A suspicion crossed her mind. "You did not challenge him?" she demanded, a good deal perturbed.

"No, but I left him no doubt that he would challenge me. He was never other than miserable with a sword."

She regarded him keenly. "I shouldn't expect he would risk being labeled a coward on a slim threat," she said.

"No, and no more would I. I imagine he has some other consideration that takes precedence over his reputation—what little of it he has left. He is retiring from society, so we may never know."

She could not be satisfied. "Why would he do that?" she asked, opening her eyes at him.

"I really left him no choice in the matter, I'm afraid. He has more to fear than facing me on the field of honor, I make no doubt."

She let go of his hands. "There is something you aren't telling," she asserted, frowning.

He smiled somewhat grimly. "Edward is an estimable secretary, my dear. Trust him to know what is going on around town. He tells me that Belderbrock's name has lately been coupled with some very odd characters indeed. Knowing this, I—shall we say—threw down the gauntlet. The question is, why did he let it lie?"

She shot a mischievous look at him. "I hope you are not going to turn into one of those odious husbands who speaks in riddles!" she said.

"My meaning will always be very clear to you, my love," he replied, sliding his hands up her arms to her shoulders. "At the moment, I am thinking of a kiss."

She gave up all attempt to look scandalized and went off into a peal of laughter. "It beats a scold," she said.

The Earl bent his head and kissed her full on her smiling mouth. "Shall we follow Belderbrock's example, and go out of town?" he suggested.

"We c-can't," she stammered, caught off guard. "We are engaged for Vauxhall Gardens tonight."

"Tomorrow then," he compromised. "I am anxious to show you Ravisham Hall."

His hopes would probably have met with little opposition, had Lady Palmer not gone to Vauxhall Gardens also. It was not that she made any push to claim the Earl's notice. Quite the opposite. She went out of her way to avoid him. Perhaps it was because she did that Adrianna could not rid herself of the notion that she stood little chance when compared with the beauty's full-blown charms. Adrianna knew all about Lady Palmer. She imagined—for there was no one to enlighten her—that all gentlemen spent every moment apart from their wives in the arms of another woman. It followed therefore that in the Earl's case, the arms belonged to Lady Palmer.

No one could have displayed greater outward spirits than Adrianna. She was gay, determinedly so, and the Earl thought her more entrancing than ever. She danced with him twice, and—correctly— once each with Lord Rockham and Mr. Perley.

She willingly accompanied the Earl to view the cascade and strolled with him along the paths, but when he suggested they visit the Lover's Walk, he found her polite and oddly reluctant. She thought of him, he mused, much as she might think of a brother. Once he took the idea into his head, he became bound to refute it. If their stalemate were to be broken, it would be up to him.

When they returned home, a candelabra was burning in the hall and a candlestick stood in readiness upon the newel post, but since the Earl did not encourage the servants to sit up for them, no one was waiting to open the door. The Earl produced his key from a pocket and fitted it into the lock. "Are you hungry?" he asked. "We could raid the larder."

"Thank you, no," she replied, following him into the house.

"A glass of Madeira, then?"

"No, nothing. Ivor, I am rather tired. If you will excuse me, I will go to bed."

"But of course, my dear," he said, walking with her to the staircase. "I will be up shortly."

She saw he was smiling faintly, and wondered at it. "At what hour do you plan to leave for Ravisham Hall?" she asked, watching him kindle a taper for her from the candelabra.

"When we wake," he replied, handing her the candle.

She placed her hand on the stair-rail preparatory to going upstairs. "Leave a call for me, please," she said. "I should hate to oversleep."

"I will wake you," he replied and turned away, leaving her staring.

Her bedroom smelt of roses. Ever after, when he smelled a rose, he would recall that night, and the bowl of them on the table beside her bed. She was lying on her side, fast asleep, with her hair streaming out across the pillows and her hands curled under her chin. In the glow of soft candlelight, one rounded breast gleamed white beneath the transparent gauze of her nightgown; seeing it, he sat down on the edge of the bed, causing her to stir and open drowsy eyes. They widened and she blanched. "Oh!" she said, sitting bolt upright.

"My dear heart!" he murmured, taking her hands in his. "My precious little love."

There was an expression in his face that brought the color rushing into her cheeks. "No!" she gasped, shrinking back. "I—I won't!"

"Why won't you?" he inquired, raising her fingers to his lips. Do you think I will make you unhappy?"

"No, but I don't want to be just—just another conquest."

His hand came under her chin and tipped it up. "Dearest," he said, "we may have contracted a marriage of convenience, you and I, but within two hours of our wedding I knew I enjoyed your company as I had not enjoyed any other female's in years. And within the course of those two days spent in that abominable little inn, I knew I had had the unbelievable good fortune to marry the one woman in the world I could not live without."

"Oh!" she breathed, blushing rosily. "How sweet you are, Ivor! How kind!"

"Sweet!" he uttered. "Kind? I assure you I am neither. I am the most selfish man alive."

"You are nothing of the sort! Why, your manners are so pretty you are even prepared to pretend when you make love to me."

"Adrianna, I could shake you. I am trying to tell you I love you, and all you can find to do is to accuse me of dissimulation."

"You cannot have fallen in love with me," she objected a trifle unsteadily. "You are used to the company of amusing, worldly women. When compared with them, I must seem dreadfully naive."

For a moment he gazed down into her face; then he let go of her hands and swept her into his arms. "Now do you understand why I want to make love to you?" he demanded, kissing her, not gently at all, but ruthlessly, tightening his arms about her until she could scarcely breathe. "I love you to the point of madness, you silly little chit."

"Oh, Ivor!" she breathed, entranced by these loverlike words. "I—I thought you loved—someone else."

"Did you indeed?" he murmured, rising to remove his robe. "You will shortly discover just how wrong you were."

Every feeling of propriety should have prompted her to avert her eyes. She did indeed blush profusely as she watched him. She stared, unable to look away. His lips curved in a knowing little

102

smile as he lay down beside her and took her in his arms.

When she woke the following morning, he was sprawled on his stomach, with an arm flung across her waist and his face pressed against her breast. Cautiously turning her head, she glanced around the room. "Oh, dear!" she thought, discovering her negligee lying on a chair some distance away. Carefully lifting his arm, it was her intent to slide out from under it, but at her first movement he stirred and opened his eyes. "You must not leave me," he admonished, raising up on one elbow. "I won't permit it."

She saw his gaze sweep her bare flesh, and pinked. "If we are leaving for Ravisham today, I should pack," she ventured.

His smile flashed. "I am unreformedly lazy, I'm afraid," he said. "I would prefer—if you don't mind, of course—to spend the day in bed."

She blinked at him, astonished. "It would create a scandal," she said.

"What?" he murmured, reaching out a hand to cup a breast.

"What w-would the servants think?" she stammered, feeling foolish.

"Oh—that," he uttered, his lips moving over her cheeks to the hollow in her throat. "Poor dear. Was it so very strange to wake and find a man in your bed?"

"Are you laughing at me?" she demanded suspiciously.

"You precious goose," he said, raising up to bend over her. "The servants are at this moment packing. We leave for Ravisham immediately following luncheon."

She made as if to rise. "I have duties—"

"Yes," he agreed, his hands moving over her with a sureness that left her limp. "Hush now, dearest, and perform them," he added, burying his face in the valley between her breasts.

Chapter 9

They set out for Ravisham Hall at shortly after two, the manner of their travel at once a surprise and a revelation to Adrianna. From thinking of the Earl as an ordinary man, his standing in the world was forcibly brought home to her. In addition to a chaise piled high with luggage, their cavalcade included the coach in which they rode, a smaller one for the servants, and several liveried outriders whose presence was more for appearances than for protection. The Earl, placid as ever, lay back in his corner and leisurely observed the emotions chasing back and forth across her face. "Quite startled, are you?" he said, amused.

She turned wide eyes on his face. "Do you always travel like this?" she asked.

"It is for your consequence, my dear," he explained. "For myself, I prefer the feel of my Arabian stallion beneath me."

"Then you must teach me to ride. I should think it a less stuffy way to move about than this."

"So I'm to turn you into a boy, am I?" he said, smiling. "Very well, my dear. But it is a girl I want in my bed, don't forget."

"A riding habit has skirts," she reminded him, chuckling.

"You will ride astride like a man. It is the only way to get the feel of your horse."

"Won't the countryside be shocked?"

"The estate covers twenty-seven thousand acres, my dear. You won't be remarked. We will explore the attics. There should be something in the trunks for you to wear."

"Then I am to be restricted to your lands?"

"No, I will teach you to ride sidesaddle as other ladies do. There are times when you will need to know. Damnable invention, the sidesaddle. You will prefer astride."

She saw his gaze drop to the V-neck of her gown dipping into the valley between her breasts, and looked away. "I have never spent any time in the country," she remarked to cover her confusion. "Will it be dreadfully dull?"

"That wasn't very complimentary to me, was it?" he laughed, reaching out an arm to pull her against his side. "Aren't we being rather shy?"

"No, of c-course not. It's just that I haven't yet become accustomed to—to—"

"You will," he murmured, parting the lace at the neck of her gown and bending his head to nuzzle at her throat.

"Ivor!" she cautioned, nodding toward the outrider stationed beside the coach.

"You are a great deal too nice," he remarked, straightening reluctantly. "How tedious it is to be good."

"Yes, that's true," she agreed, the severity of her expression somewhat belied by the twinkle in her eyes. "Tell me about Ravisham Hall. Is it large?"

"Quite large. Some of it is very old. It is shaped like the letter *H*, and the center part, or crossbar, has stood for nearly four hundred years. I think you will enjoy the view. It is situated on a rise of ground, you know. On a clear day one can see the Roman ruins."

"It sounds intriguing," she said, a rapt expression coming on her face. "Have you explored the ruins?"

"Many times," he said indulgently. "We will bespeak an early dinner one evening, and I will take you there. It is particularly impressive in the moonlight."

In her opinion, Ravisham Hall itself proved impressive enough to startle strangers coming upon it unawares. First appearing as a vast mass upon the distant horizon, it next assumed the lines of a fortress, and only took on the aura of a home as they drew near. Built of stone, and austere in line, it needed the ivy clinging to its walls to bring it into a dimension habitable by man. All was bustle and confusion when their cavalcade pulled into the courtyard and came to a standstill before the recessed entry-way. The door of the coach was pulled open, the steps were let down, and the Earl descended to the ground, a black scowl upon his brow. Adrianna, leaning forward to view this oldest portion of the house, was at once struck by a feeling of having arrived back in the far distant past. She could almost visualize in her mind's eye the sight of knights in armor riding forth to do battle in defense of a lady's honor. The Earl's stretching out a hand to assist her chased away the thought. Stepping forth, she was surprised to see any number of strange coaches in the courtyard from which luggage was being unloaded and carried inside. "Have we guests?" she asked, going with him toward the door.

"It appears so," he replied, mouth grim. "My Aunts Alvy, Bertelda, Clusty, and Doyle."

Her delighted laugh rang out. "What, no E?" she said.

"Aunt Esselry died in infancy. Apparently Aunt Flournoy has yet to arrive. I'm sorry, sweet. Shall we return to London before they know we're here?"

"You know we cannot have them think I despise

their acquaintance. And besides, how often does one have an opportunity to greet the alphabet?"

"Had they been boys, Grandmother would have named them Matthew, Mark, Luke, and John."

Again her delighted chuckle rang out. "I do wish I could have known your grandmother," she said. "She sounds like fun."

"Perhaps a ditty will help you keep the aunts straight. How's this? A stands for aloof, B is for beware, C is only childish, while D can spell despair."

"And F?" she gurgled.

"Frightful," he said. "What else?"

"I know what it is," she said. "You would have me believe you come from an unusual family, but one has to draw the line somewhere."

"You will know better the first time Aunt Bertelda utters her thoughts aloud," he remarked, leading her into the paneled hall. "'Beware' describes her tongue exactly."

She was struck at once by the sense of history in the armor and ancient weapons displayed against the walls. She would have liked to tour the house, but Lady Bertelda appeared in an open archway at the far end of the room, claiming Adrianna's attention. She was a woman of some beauty and a fair amount of wit; that she seemed vague was due entirely to vanity. Between being extremely nearsighted, and refusing to wear glasses, she seldom knew to whom she spoke. "Dear me!" she said, squinting. "Visitors!"

"Is it Ravisham, dear?" a voice called through the open door.

The Earl placed a hand beneath Adrianna's elbow and led her forward. "What a pleasant surprise, Auntie B," he said with an irony that went completely over her head.

"Dear boy, and so this is your wife," she said, discovering Adrianna by his side. "Come into the study, dear ones. Sisters are waiting."

Indeed they were. Adrianna soon determined that Auntie A was painfully shy, and of a kindly disposition. Auntie C, the childish one, seemed more infantile than spoiled. Of the four of them, Adrianna felt most drawn to Auntie D. If she did sometimes despair, it was clear she probably had cause. Thirty minutes in their assorted company left Adrianna with one thought in mind: escape. It wasn't that she didn't like them well enough. She was bored, and so was the Earl.

"I wonder what is keeping dearest Flournoy," Auntie B said suddenly. "She would have it that Ravisham could do with our support. And such a beauty too! It's a pity!"

"As I said: beware," the Earl remarked, the devil in his smiling eyes.

Adrianna tried to maintain her composure and failed, going off into a peal of laughter.

The Earl turned back to his aunt, brows raised. "The gathering of the clan?" he said.

"You know how Flournoy is," Auntie B replied. "And such a handsome man! I knew his father well."

"Oh?" said the Earl. "Is Auntie F contemplating matrimony?"

Auntie C giggled, but the others looked scandalized. "Flournoy marry Viscount Shirley?" Auntie D inquired. "Wherever did you get that idea?"

"Shirley?" the Earl said, looking surprised. "What has he to do with Auntie F?"

"Not with Flournoy, dear boy. Oh, dear me, no!"

"It's that woman," Auntie B explained. "I hate to say it, Ravisham, but you should have waited until your marriage to bestow your notice."

"Now, Auntie B," the Earl admonished, glancing at Adrianna.

"It is not quite clear in my mind," she continued, "but I expect that horrid will of Cousin William is at the bottom of it all."

Auntie D sniffed. "You know perfectly well, Bertelda, that Ravisham didn't need Cousin William's money. His wealth was already sufficient to attract the wrong sort of woman."

"Doyle is feeling peevish," Auntie A explained. "Flournoy practically ordered us to come here, but that is in her usual way."

"Just what did she say?" the Earl asked.

"It seems that Lady Palmer made some remark in Viscount Shirley's hearing that led him to believe she had posted a missive to you," Auntie B replied. "Had she?"

"I know of no reason why she should."

"Viscount Shirley paid a call in Cavendish Square last evening—and at a very late hour, dear me, yes. Lady Palmer had left him with the impression that she stands much in your debt. Does she?"

"Shirley is a fount of information," the Earl remarked dryly, ignoring the question.

"Adrianna would rather be resting in her rooms, I daresay," Auntie C remarked, entering the lists. "I am sure she must be acquiring a poor impression of us," she added with an insight unexpected by her relations.

"No, no!" Adrianna exclaimed. "I am sure—"

"We grieved so at being unable to attend your wedding, but with Major Gilroy's tragic death, and then the funeral—he was family, you know—well, we did so want you to see us at our best."

"Do not distress yourself," the Earl said, gently swinging his quizzing-glass to and fro. "Adrianna knows all about my past indiscretions."

Adrianna only seemed amused. "Certainly I do," she said. "I trust you do not intend, at this late date, to speak of it. It would quite set your aunts on end."

Aunie A folded her needlework and laid it aside. "Dearest Ravisham has long tended to do so," she remarked. "I daresay he may now grow more dependable with a woman's hand to guide him."

The Earl rose. "Don't put ideas into Adrianna's head," he chuckled, strolling toward the door. "I presume you still enjoy a glass of wine before dinner? We will join you then. Come along, Adrianna. I have something to show you."

She assumed he would conduct her over the house, but he led her outside through the door of an anteroom at the back of the house. "How lovely!" she murmured, gazing around at the gardens, then gasped when he seized her hand and strode off down a path in the shrubbery toward the stable yard beyond. "I would be obliged if you will cease dragging me along like some horrid mule! Will you unhand me, you wretch!"

"No, little craven, I won't," he grinned, quickening his stride.

"Odious creature!" she retorted, practically running to keep up. "It had better be good!"

"It is," he replied, taking her through the great double doors into the stable.

It smelled of sweat and horses and new-mown hay. Adrianna, entranced, moved from stall to stall, crooning to the horses and stroking their velvety noses. She knew the magnificent Arabian must be the Earl's favorite the instant she paused before him. "He's sweet," she said.

"Sweet!" he repeated, grinning at her. "He has the devil's own temper when he chooses."

"I expect it's you," she retorted, trying to look smug, and failing. "Put me up on his back, Ivor, please."

"The deuce you say!" he replied, startled. "He'd have you off in a trice."

"Of all the unhandsome things to say! He is a perfect gentleman. I can tell."

"Can you now? Well, my dear, you know nothing of brutes, if you think that."

"I know all about brutes," she shot back, a little smile teasing her lips. "You hope to fob me off, but it will not do!"

He looked at her in a measuring way. "I'm tempted," he said. "Don't press your luck. As it is,

I had best inform the grooms not to let you near him. His hooves—"

"Very well. You need say no more," she interrupted. "Just don't think to put me aboard some rubbishing slug. I may not know how to ride but I do know what I will ride. I have very definite ideas about that!"

"Don't look so put-upon," he smiled. "From what I know of you, I would wager a goodly sum on the certainty that you will ride to an inch before the week is out."

"That's as may be, but you have yet to show me which of these horses I'm to ride."

"This one," he said, opening the door to the third stall on the right.

"She is certainly not sluggish," she remarked, watching him lead the mare out to the center of the floor.

His brows rose. "How did you know she is a she?" he said, surprised.

"She has a dainty step," she replied, moving forward.

"All thoroughbreds have," he remarked. "No, Adrianna. Come around to the other side. Always mount on the left."

"How on earth do you expect me to get all the way up there?" she asked, eyeing the mare askance.

"Put your foot in my cupped hands," he said. "That's it. Careful now. Just sit still and get the feel of it."

"It seems such a long way to the ground," she remarked, smiling down at him.

113

"Sit erect in the saddle, sweet. Keep your chin up and your elbows in."

"I haven't a saddle," she giggled, leaning forward to pat the long neck.

"Pretend," he replied, grasping the mare by her mane. "I'm going to walk her up and down. Do try not to fall off."

"Will you catch me if I do?" she asked, feeling some slight trepidation.

"Don't bounce around so," he said, ignoring the question. "Squeeze her flanks with your knees. No, Adrianna. You're jiggling. Try to move with the horse."

"I know I'm bouncing up and down," she said, biting her lip. "I can't help it."

"Yes, you can. Relax. Let the animal do the work."

"I'm trying," she said, wincing. "It hurts my— my posterior."

"Tomorrow you will use a saddle," he promised, holding out his arms. "Well, come on down. That is enough for now."

"Thank goodness for that!" she said, slipping into his grasp, relieved. "I should hate to eat my dinner standing up. It would only give you an opening to say something outrageous."

He was smiling, but as her body slid downward along his lean frame, she saw his nostrils flare and heard the sharp intake of his breath. The next instant a merry whistle announced the approach of a groom, and he released her, turning away to restore the mare to her stall. He did not forget to exchange a pleasantry with the stable-hand before rushing Adrianna somewhat precipitately to the house. She looked at him in surprise, but offered no comment until he ushered her into the sitting room of a suite taking up the entire first floor of the east wing. "Later," he said, putting his arms around her. "You can see it later."

"Why not now?" she asked, eyes round.

"No!" he said, kissing her, gently at first, then deeply. The heat rising in him, he strained her to him hungrily, demanding a response to his passion that she was glad to give. He sat down on the edge of the bed and pulled her forward into his arms until her breasts were pressed against his face. "You are so beautiful, my dearest love," he whispered. "So very, very beautiful. Say you love me!"

"I do love you, Ivor," she murmured, caught up in the thrill of his seeking lips and searching hands. His mouth pressed against the hollow of her throat. Gasping, she clasped her hands behind his head and held him close.

Afterward he could hardly believe that she was his. Loving her beyond reason, and knowing she felt the same, he felt humbled and elated at the same time.

"It would be interesting to know what is passing through your brain," he said.

"Poor idiot," she replied, turning the word into a caress. "It would be useless to tell you. You wouldn't understand."

"Try me," he murmured, carrying her fingers to his lips.

"You are selfish and indolent, for all your

115

amiability. I suppose it is useless to think you might put yourself out for anyone."

"My tongue is not the only deadly scourge in this family," he remarked appreciatively. "What have I done to deserve a lashing?"

She laughed and said, "You let me keep you from making love to me. And positively for weeks, too."

"Yes," he agreed, his lips quivering. "I think I may be said to have let you do that."

"Why did you?" she demanded. "You should have forced me."

"There is nothing for it, my darling," he said, lifting a hand to tweak her nose. "I shall have to make love to you again. You would have scratched out my eyes."

"The thing is, Ivor, I don't believe you sought —well, consolation in Lady Palmer's arms. Not after we were married, at least."

"For God's sake, Adrianna!" he ejaculated in quick exasperation. "Of all the things to say!"

"Surely you don't want me to read you a list of the reasons why I have nothing to fear from her?"

"No, spare me that, at least."

"Well, but I always thought that married couples should—should talk about things."

"The things you elect to discuss, my pet, are reprehensible in the extreme."

"Don't be silly," she said. "From what I have seen thus far, we will need a united front if we are to face down your Aunt Flournoy. Promise me you will share Lady Palmer's letter with me."

"That depends. I may have been a rake, but there are limits beyond which I refuse to go."

"But if it isn't personal, you will?"

"I can promise you that, yes."

"I expect it isn't. Your manners would have prompted you to part with her on the best of terms. One's ex-mistress can be an asset if she feels friendly toward one. She is bound to enjoy the confidence of other men."

"Even such an accolade as that fails to awaken any desire in me to pursue the subject," he said dryly. "If I had had any presence of mind at all, I would have rushed you upstairs before you had opportunity for discourse with my aunts."

"I hope you are not offended, but I thought we should come to a meeting of the minds."

"But I am offended, and there is only one cure for that!"

It seemed to Adrianna that he fairly swooped on her. She was swept into a crushing embrace and ruthlessly kissed. "Well!" he demanded. "Are you going to concentrate on me?"

Adrianna, quite cowed by such treatment, meekly nodded and put her arms around his neck.

Chapter 10

At about the same time that the Earl and Adrianna had left London that day, Lord Belderbrock was admitted into a house in Curzon Street. Informed that Lord Chester was engaged, there was nothing he could do but kick his heels in the drawing room and mentally rephrase all that he intended to say. The tall clock in the corner had just struck three when a footman appeared and escorted him across the hall to the study overlooking the street, where his lordship was awaiting him in frowning silence.

Lord Chester, who was seated behind a mahogany desk with an open ledger before him and a stack of papers ready for his signature at his elbow, cast him an unfriendly glance and told the footman he did not wish to be disturbed. "Well, my dear Belderbrock," he said after allowing a full minute to elapse following the door's closing behind the servant.

Lord Belderbrock moistened his lips and forced himself to meet a pair of coldly uncompromising eyes. "I—why, the fact of the matter is, I—my expenses—"

"I trust they are within your capacity to pay," Lord Chester interrupted.

Belderbrock shifted his feet, acutely aware that he had not been invited to sit. "If results are to accrue—"

"At the moment," said his lordship, "I have yet to ascertain any results at all."

"You will," Belderbrock assured him, nervously clearing his throat. "I have impressed Grimcoe with the necessity for recovering the letters at once."

"I am glad to find that you realize the need for speed," his lordship remarked. "I was beginning to think that you did not."

"Of course I do. Ravisham may be considered a heedless exquisite in some quarters, but for myself I have always believed a keen mind lurked behind that weary manner he chooses to adopt."

"Your perspicacity overwhelms me," Lord Chester said dryly. "I hadn't thought you had it in you."

Lord Belderbrock stiffened. "Whatever can you mean?" he demanded, blustering.

Lord Chester leaned back in his chair and cooly looked him over. "I am unaware of having couched my meaning in obscure terms," he said.

"I told you in the beginning that Lord Ravisham is not a man to fool with."

"And so I told Grimcoe. It is only a matter of providing an additional sum to defray his expenses."

"He has had all he will get from me," Lord Chester replied in a tone Lord Belderbrock could only find offensive.

Belderbrock flushed. "You can't refuse to advance a paltry amount!" he said, aghast to find himself begging.

"Ah, but I was under the impression that I could," his lordship replied bluntly.

"But—but that would mean it would come out of my share!" Belderbrock sputtered.

"Precisely," his lordship agreed.

"And where am I to get the money?" Belderbrock demanded. "You know very well my pockets are to let!"

"That is your problem, surely. You have all my sympathy, but I have already put up my share."

"Well, if that's your final answer, I'm in the devil of a fix. I will need to go to a moneylender."

Lord Chester once more looked Belderbrock over in a way that made him cringe. "Indeed you shan't, you fool," he said. "Do you want such as they nosing about our business? You have bungled enough as it is."

"It wasn't my fault Grimcoe hid the letters at Twinfriars," Belderbrock protested, blanching. If it came to a choice between the Earl and Lord Chester, he would rather face the Earl.

"In God's name, why Twinfriars?" Lord Chester demanded suddenly.

"It is a secluded spot; his lordship rarely ventured from the house, and certainly few people had called there in years. It seemed ideal."

"Seemed! You must be very dull-witted!"

Very white about the lips, Lord Belderbrock sank uninvited into a chair. "Grimcoe had been attending his lordship of an evening, expecting to be paid. He had no idea the old goat would die!"

"I don't see what that signifies. The letters were out of our control."

"No, there was no likelihood Lord William would have the paintings removed from his walls. He fairly doted on them, Grimcoe tells me."

"It seems my destiny to be surrounded by fools," Lord Chester remarked to the room at large. "They could have been stolen, you idiot!"

"No one but Grimcoe and the Chitterings knew that they were there," Belderbrock explained. "And Chittering had no idea they were valuable."

"Indeed?" said Lord Chester, turning a quill between his fingers. "And if he found out?"

"There is a way to enter the house unseen. Grimcoe stumbled upon a door hidden behind overgrown shrubbery when walking in the gardens one evening. He could have retrieved the letters at any time we chose."

"Could he?" Lord Chester said in a voice that chilled Lord Belderbrock to the marrow.

"It—it was all so—unforeseen. Grimcoe had no

idea that Lady Ravisham was sleeping in his lordship's room."

"No, of course he wouldn't," Lord Chester remarked.

"At least he had not yet slit the paper protecting the back of the Rubens!"

"How comforting," Lord Chester murmured, his eyes cold as steel.

Lord Belderbrock swallowed the lump in his throat. "She believed his explanation, never fear," he said with what assurance he could summon.

"Ah, but I do fear," Lord Chester replied in silken tones, "I find myself dwelling upon the punishment meted out in such cases in the past. It is blackmail, you fool!"

"I could not have known that Ravisham would remove the paintings to London," he protested. "In the circumstances, Grimcoe need only break into Ravisham House to retrieve the letters. The Earl and Countess have left for Ravisham Hall."

"When I brought you into my plans, I would never have dreamed that evidence worth a fortune would be secreted in the back of a painting which neither of us even owns!"

"You mean to put the blame on me. My position—"

"It would surprise me very much if you understand your position," Lord Chester said, studying Lord Belderbrock from under drooping lids. "Grimcoe is your hireling. There is nothing, nothing at all, to connect me with the crime. Do I make myself clear?"

"Sir!" Belderbrock ejaculated, stunned.

"Nothing! My butler informed me you very properly arrived here today in a hired hackney. You will, I trust, not venture to come here again. I need only add that it is not unknown for dead bodies to turn up in the most unlikely places."

"You mean—m-murder?" Lord Belderbrock gasped.

"Labels can be so incriminating," Lord Chester remarked, the smile not quite reaching his eyes. "I never employ them."

"I shan't—you cannot mean—"

"When I find an obstacle in my path, I am apt to remove it. However, for so long as Grimcoe remains ignorant of my involvement, you have nothing to fear. Unless, of course, you fail to uphold your end of our bargain. Now get out, and don't contact me again until you have the letters in your hands."

Lord Belderbrock rose on trembling legs. "You pretend to great respectability, my lord, but I know of your gaming debts," he surprised himself by saying.

Lord Chester smiled. "Even so," he said, "I am not fool enough to have incriminating evidence in my possession."

Lord Belderbrock could think of nothing more to say. Feeling kinship with the fly caught in a spider's web, he got himself from the room with as much dignity as he could muster and set off on foot for home, muttering under his breath and vainly searching his mind for some possibility of revenge.

* * *

At Ravisham Hall two mornings later, Adrianna finished tucking her hair under a cap, and critically surveyed her reflection in the long mirror. Entranced with her appearance, she chuckled and went in search of the Earl, locating him in his dressing room. "I think I really do look like a boy," she remarked, strutting up and down for his inspection.

"You look the most complete tatterdemalion imaginable," he said, amusement gleaming in his eyes. "Whatever have you done to that cravat?"

"I tied it," she said with some defiance.

"That is obvious," he replied. "Something tells me I should have left well enough alone."

"Well, I am glad your nanny saved all your outgrown clothes. I like wearing breeches. They do not restrict one's movements as skirts do."

"Depraved we both may be," he replied, "but for heaven's sake keep your hair tucked out of sight in case we come across someone. You might also remove that cravat."

"No, I like it," she said. "And besides, it's becoming."

He laughed. "Then come here and let me see what I can do," he said.

"I hope you have a saddle that is small enough for me," she remarked, standing still while he struggled futilely with the cloth inexpertly bound around her throat.

"You may use one I had as a youth," he replied, removing the crumpled folds and reaching for a clean cravat.

"Is anything ever thrown away at Ravisham?" she asked, craning her neck to catch a glimpse of his fingers performing magic with the fresh neckcloth.

"Seldom," he said. "There, that is much better. At least you no longer resemble a scrubby brat."

"No, I don't, do I?" she said, pleased with this accolade. "I could easily be taken for a young gentleman of fashion sent down from school for—for—for smuggling a serving girl into my quarters!" she finished on a triumphant note.

"No boys' school would be foolish enough to hire female servants," he informed her. "And kindly unbutton that coat. Now that I look at you more precisely, I can tell you that no 'young gentleman of fashion' would possess two enticing bulges at that particular location on his anatomy."

"I thought you said no one would remark me while I am riding on your lands," she muttered, unfastening the clasps of the jacket.

"Don't remind me of that, please," he said, grinning. "I am as reprehensible as you. Now I come to think of it, you had best remain aboard your horse. No young lad would possess rounded feminine hips either."

Her eyes twinkled. "You know," she said, "I have been thinking, and I have come up with a capital idea! If we go down to breakfast now, all of your aunts are bound to be at table, now that Aunt Flournoy has arrived. We would never get away."

"Are you proposing I go without my meal?" he said, brows raised. "For if you are, I will inform

125

you I become cross as a bear when deprived of it."

"No, no, of course I did not mean that!" she assured him. "We will breakfast at some inn."

"Am I to understand you propose deliberately flaunting yourself abroad?" he asked.

"No one would know," she said. "They haven't seen me."

"And if they guessed?"

"They wouldn't. Not if we are clever. Please, Ivor. Do let's! It would be such fun!"

He sighed and rose. "I should shudder at the mere thought of it," he said. "Why, oh why, did I offer to teach you to ride astride! My own conduct is becoming a scandal."

This remark had the effect of causing her to giggle and say, "I have been thinking about how we should leave the house. It seems to me we had best go by the back stairs if we are to avoid being seen."

"Your brain has been busy," he remarked, his eyes dwelling on the animated face turned up to him. "Well, come along. The back stairs will do nicely for a pair of wicked adventurers let loose upon the world."

In a spirit of pure mischief, Adrianna slipped her hand in his and crept with him from the room.

The head groom had been in the Earl's service for too many years to evince surprise. If his lordship cared little for her ladyship's consequence, it was not for him to say. The only sign of disapproval he permitted himself was a tightening of the lips when he placed the saddle the Earl had used when a child on the mare's back, and tightened the girth. He knew very well what his lordship's late mother would have thought. Breeches, indeed!

Adrianna, blithely unaware of the elderly retainer's unfavorable opinion of her attire, allowed the Earl to toss her into the saddle, struggled to remain upright, and smiled her gratitude when he reached out an arm to steady her. "What do I do with my feet?" she asked, picking up the reins and watching him swing aboard the stallion.

"Put them into the stirrups. Those things dangling from your saddle. Careful, Adrianna! Don't kick her flanks. We will go slowly until you get the feel of it."

They rode sedately out of the stable yard and on down the carriage-way, a curve in the drive soon hiding them from sight of the house. "I feel more confident every minute," she observed. "I think I'm right good at this."

"You draw a pretty picture, my dear," he replied, smiling, "but you are far from being a proper equestrienne. Keep your back straight and your elbows in."

"I learn quickly. You'll see."

"You will progress at the pace I set for you, my love. First we walk, and then we trot. You will not gallop until I say you may."

She laughed. "So you are going to be a tyrant," she said.

"You wanted me to teach you, remember. You must expect to reap the harvest of your own sowing."

"I imagine I will know better in future," she gurgled, cutting her eyes at him. "A husband makes a very poor tutor."

"You think so?" he grinned, his eyes running over her in a way that imparted a meaning she could not miss.

They had not more than a mile and a half to go to the inn on the main road to Brampton, but due to the slowness of their pace, it was after ten o'clock before they reached it. Being situated on the main highway, it was an ancient hostelry, half-timbered, with a thatched roof. The Earl swung down from his stallion and, after admonishing Adrianna to wait, strode inside. Returning almost immediately, he told her that they were in luck, no patrons were about. "I took the liberty of ordering bacon and eggs, if this meets with your approval," he added, holding up his arms to assist her to the ground.

It did. "What name will you give, should anyone ask?" she said, going with him inside.

"My own," he replied. "Why?"

"I think it would be romantic to falsely identify ourselves. Don't you?"

"No."

"Well, that is certainly being brief. Why not?"

"Should someone who knows me happen by, I would be made to look extremely foolish."

She cast him a teasing look. "If you ask me," she said, "you will give away our secret if you are seen holding my chair for me."

"You have the most audacious tongue of anyone of my total acquaintance," he remarked, shoving her into her seat none too gently.

"Much better," she approved, twinkling up at him. "Do you know what I think, Ivor?"

"Probably," he said, sitting down.

"Well, it is my belief you would make a very good conspirator, if you put your mind to it."

"I will confess that aspect of our adventure had not occurred to me. I had not known we were —er, conspiring."

"Oh?" she said. "I see. What did you think we were doing, if I may ask?"

"Having breakfast."

"We could pretend I'm your cousin," she suggested, propping her chin on her cupped hands and gazing at him with no little expectation.

"I have no cousin," he replied in some amusement.

"A nephew?" she said hopefully.

"I have no scruffy male relations at all," he said, adding succinctly, "young or old."

The landlord came into the room at that moment, followed by his wife bearing their breakfast on a tray, making further comment impossible. It was apparent that he was mystified. The Earl was properly attired for riding in buckskin breeches, top-boots, and a plain coat, but the cut of his coat and the shine on his boots proclaimed him a gentleman of considerable wealth, and possibly of rank. Inquisitiveness overcame the better part of discretion. "Is your lordship from these parts?" he asked, taking their plates from the tray and placing them upon the table.

"I am Ravisham," the Earl replied calmly, causing the landlord to goggle.

"Of Ravisham Hall," Adrianna added helpfully. "I am the orphaned son of a deceased friend of his lordship."

The landlady was immediately all sympathy. "You poor child," she murmured, gazing at Adrianna in a motherly way. "Was your bereavement of a recent date?"

Adrianna cast down her eyes. "Tolerably so," she said without a moment's hesitation.

The landlord turned to the Earl. "Has he come to live with your lordship?" he asked, folding his hands before his ample girth and waiting expectantly for the Earl's reply.

"Something of the sort," the Earl answered blandly. "Do sit up straight, Edward," he added to Adrianna. "I have told you repeatedly it is ill-mannered to lean your elbows upon the table."

"I forgot," Adrianna muttered, enjoying herself immensely.

"That's the trouble with young gentlemen today," the landlord said to the Earl. "No manners. They need the seat of their breeches dusted, is what I say. Will your lordship care for anything more?"

Upon being replied to in the negative, the landlord bowed and, followed by his spouse dropping agitated little curtsies, left the room. "Of course you would be newly orphaned," the Earl remarked the instant the door closed behind them.

"Well, I shouldn't wish irate parents appearing

upon the scene to whisk me away from you," she said with a perfectly straight face.

"May I ask why they would be irate? No, on second thought, don't answer that. I think I prefer not to know."

She gave her entrancing little gurgle of laughter. "Are you irate?" she said.

"Yes," he admitted. "Do you mind?"

"No, not at all," she replied. "You are laughing irate. That is a good deal different from being frowning irate."

His lips twitched. "Eat your breakfast," he said.

The clatter of horses' hooves on the cobblestoned courtyard out front was heard at this moment, followed shortly by a hasty step entering the inn, and a voice raised in shouted summons of the landlord. "Good God!" the Earl ejaculated, laying down his knife and fork.

"Who is it?" Adrianna asked, turning her face toward the sounds of muffled speech reaching them from the entry-way.

"A friend of mine. Of all the damnable luck!"

Adrianna had no trouble at all in recognizing their difficulty. She would have given all she possessed to be garbed in a proper habit; as it was, she could only shrink down in her chair and attempt to efface herself.

The door was flung open, and a gentleman in a fifteen-cape driving coat of white drab cloth strode in. "Ravisham, of all people!" he said, seizing the Earl's hand and pumping it. "I was on my way to the Hall when my off-leader threw a shoe.

131

What in the name of all that's holy are you doing here?"

"Eating my breakfast," the Earl replied. "Will you care to join us?"

"Eh?" Lord Charles exclaimed, discovering Adrianna, and staring.

"The trifling son of a deceased friend of mine," the Earl explained with perfect aplomb. "Edward, say hello to Lord Jaimie Charles."

Adrianna blushed, half rose from her chair, and then sank back down, mumbling an inaudible greeting.

"Edward who?" said Lord Charles.

"Er—Hunt," replied the Earl.

"You, a cub-leader?" Lord Charles demanded. "I don't believe it. It ain't like you, Ravisham."

"I quite agree."

"Another thing. You haven't a deceased friend. I ain't one to moralize, but—"

Had Adrianna's eyes not been on the Earl's face, she would have missed his slightly heightened color. "Don't be an ass," he said, pulling off Adrianna's cap and letting her hair come tumbling down around her shoulders. "I doubt she desires your acquaintance, Jaimie, but civility requires the introduction. I beg leave to present my wife, the Countess of Ravisham."

Lord Charles started. "Good God!" he exclaimed, appalled. "Ma'am, it's an honor. I didn't mean— Lord! What can I say?"

"You have already said too much," the Earl remarked. "A simple hello will suffice."

"I've a very good mind to go out and come

back in again," Lord Charles replied, favoring Adrianna with a winning smile. "I wouldn't bungle it a second time."

Adrianna held out her hand. "You are less at fault than I, sir," she said. "How do you do. I usually wear skirts, by the way."

"Shall we both cease agonizing?" he grinned, bowing over her hand with an easy grace. "You are lovely in any guise."

"You had better let well enough alone, Jaimie," the Earl remarked. "Tell me why you wished to see me."

"Oh, that!" Lord Charles groaned. "I am in the devil of a fix. Run clean off my legs, in fact."

"I see," the Earl sighed, reaching into his pocket. "I'm afraid I haven't much on me at the moment. How much—"

"No, no, put it away," Lord Charles interrupted. "I do appreciate it, but a few pounds won't solve my problem this time. I don't know what the deuce to do."

"I take it that it is serious?"

"Yes. Oh, God, yes. Damn it—excuse me, ma'am. I'll tell you what, Ivor, I'm in no fit case to converse before a lady."

"Then you will reserve your revelations for the privacy of my study. I do wish you will take a cup of coffee, dear boy. I promise you we will return home immediately we finish breakfast."

Chapter 11

Arrived back at Ravisham Hall, and informed by the butler that Lord Charles had been shown into his study, the Earl watched Adrianna ascend the stairs to don feminine attire before strolling away to join his guest. From the looks of it, his lordship had beguiled the waiting by pouring himself several drinks and tossing them off. "Dear me," said the Earl, gazing at Lord Charles in some surprise. "We are in sad case."

His lordship's cravat seemed too tight. Reaching up a hand, he jerked it loose. "The worst!" he groaned. "I am being blackmailed!"

The Earl put up his quizzing-glass and surveyed his friend through it. "Tell me about it," he said calmly.

"The oldest trick in the books, and I fell for it."

The eyeglass dropped "A female, I take it," the Earl remarked. "Really, old boy."

"She seemed so—so sweet and pure."

"They always do. Don't tell me you took pen in hand?"

"How did you guess?" Lord Charles muttered, staring.

"I take it you promised eternal devotion. How many letters, if you don't mind?"

"Five or six. I forget which. M'father would have my hide if I married the wench."

"I should rather think he would. Have you contacted the police?"

"I can't, old boy. Papa would be sure to get wind of it. Twenty thousand, mark you! To tell you the truth, Ivor, I wouldn't turn over twenty thousand pounds to a scurvy blackmailer if I had it. Which I don't. Not the thing. Not the thing at all. He would only come back for more."

"He?"

"Well, it stands to reason. Lottie—that's the girl's name—Lottie can only be described as dumb. Fascinating, but dumb."

"The two naturally go together," the Earl remarked, amused. "Since you do not care to involve the law, presumably you have reason to believe you can resolve the matter with no one the wiser."

"By no means. The fact is, I need your help to bring it off. You know Lord Belderbrock quite well, I hear."

"Not well, no."

"The devil you say! He has put it all about that you do. I'll tell you what, Ivor: He's a loose-screw."

"I agree. What brought him to your mind?"

"He delivered the blackmailer's demand. Said a young lad accosted him in the street; said the boy had been paid to ask him to pass along this missive to me," Lord Charles said, fishing a grubby piece of paper from a pocket and holding it out. "It's a queer start, if you want my opinion."

The Earl gingerly took the sheet of scrawled handwriting between finger and thumb, and perused it. "Ungrammatical, but clear," he remarked. "Our blackmailer is either poorly educated, or he finds it expedient to appear as if he is. One thing is sure. He has clearly masked his hand."

"That's what I thought. No one writes as sloppy as that."

"It has just crossed my mind that we may possibly be dealing with more than one man. If Belderbrock was in it alone, he would have hired an accomplice to deliver the note. That he did not suggests at least two additional men mixed up in the affair: our poorly educated friend, and a third who was too wise to rely entirely upon either an ignoramus or a fool. Thus he remains anonymous, while Belderbrock accomplishes a contact impossible to the third."

Lord Charles cocked an eyebrow. "In case you are right, it's worse than I thought. We haven't a clue whom to watch."

"Oh, I imagine that hasn't changed," the Earl said placidly. "Belderbrock is still our man. Given time, he will surely blunder. Set that sly little cockney tiger of yours to watch him, and let nature do the rest."

"I knew you'd help me, Ivor, but I never dreamed you would put my mind to rest so fast. Damn if this doesn't call for a drink."

"By all means. Make mine brandy, if you please."

Having poured out two glasses from a decanter on the table, Lord Charles handed the Earl one of them and returned to his chair before the fire. "I fancy I may have slipped a peg before your wife," he began, stretching out his legs. "Sorry, old boy. I wouldn't have, not for the world."

"I fancy Adrianna hadn't a clue. Forget it."

"At the risk of getting my ears pinned back for my pains, answer me this: just what was she doing rigged out in your old breeches?"

"That was my notion, I'm afraid," the Earl admitted. "She has never learned to ride, so I have undertaken to teach her."

"Astride?" Lord Charles demanded, much struck.

"But of course astride, dear boy," the Earl replied, amused.

"Well, if that don't beat all!" Lord Charles gasped, gazing at him open-mouthed. "I never dreamt you had it in you."

"Do try not to be hidebound, Jaimie. How else is she to get the feel of her horse?"

Lord Charles gave a sudden shout of laughter. "Gad, but I'd like to be on hand when that hatchet-faced old aunt of yours gets wind of this," he said, mopping his eyes. "It ain't fitting in a man of fashion. Damn if it is!"

"Kindly keep your voice down," the Earl said

dryly. "You may not mind Aunt Flournoy's strictures, but I can assure that I do."

Lord Charles sat bolt upright. "Never tell me she's in the house!" he gasped, casting the Earl a startled look.

"She is," the Earl replied, taking snuff.

A terrible premonition seized Lord Charles. "Not all five of them?" he begged, his face comic with dismay.

"Sorry," the Earl murmured apologetically.

"Then I'll be off," Lord Charles declared, surging to his feet. "No offense, old boy, but I'll be damned if I'll sit down to luncheon with one of 'em shouting in my ear, while another of them shrinks back every time I look at her."

The Earl smiled. "You will miss seeing Aunt Flournoy's face," he said.

An unholy gleam stole into Lord Charles's eyes. "You are in the devil of a fix," he said, clapping the Earl upon the back. "It ain't that I'm craven, but I'll let you tell me about it the next time I see you."

But the Earl was not destined to receive a dressing down. Lady Flournoy, having discovered that he had returned, waited only until the front door closed behind Lord Charles to make her way to the Earl's study. "I must say I cannot find favor with your conduct," she announced the instant she entered the room.

The Earl gave a short laugh and rose from the chair behind his desk. "Dear me," he said. "Did you come to tell me that?"

"It does you scant credit, certainly," she replied, running an eye over his hard frame. "In my salad days, a gentleman donned morning clothing in the morning."

"I have just a short time ago returned from riding. But you did not come to talk about my clothes. How may I serve you?"

"Do not be disdainful with me, Ravisham. It leaves me supremely indifferent. I have been put to a good deal of trouble on your behalf, as have my sisters."

"I am sorry to have offended you, Auntie F. May I ring for tea?"

"Sit down, boy. What I have to say is of grave importance."

"Then by all means," he replied, walking around his desk and taking a chair facing hers.

"I don't know what you have been about, to send Lady Palmer looking all over town for you," she began without preamble. "I knew nothing of it until she came seeking you in Cavendish Square."

His eyes met hers for an instant. "Are you quite sure?" he said, glancing away.

"Do not pretend with me, Ravisham. There can be no mistake. She came around to me after knocking on your door. Perhaps you think I am needlessly alarmed, but I have spoken with Simpson. No, you need not think he said anything of which you would disapprove. I am sure no butler of yours would consider giving you away."

"Give me away in what?" the Earl asked, startled.

"Your affair with that hussy. Pray do not dissemble."

"You are entirely mistaken, Auntie F. It ceased upon my marriage. I cannot imagine what she could want with me. Just what did she say?"

"I scarcely know what she said. Something about debts of friendship, and needing to let you know. Really, Ravisham, she made no sense at all. None in the least."

"I'm afraid I cannot enlighten you," he said. "From my knowledge of her, I shouldn't think it important. She was always excitable, you know."

"No, I do not know. I think you should go up to London to see what is to be done. You can't have her making inquiries about you all over town. You do see the need for discretion on her part, I'm sure. She will set the whole world talking."

"Let me handle it, Auntie F. I should not, if I were you, discuss the matter with anyone. It could not help, and might do harm. Or have you? Is that why the aunts are here?"

"We are here to lend you countenance. No one would give credence to gossip with us to refute it."

"I rather think they wouldn't dare," he remarked with the glimmer of a smile.

He was not without hope that a few days spent at Ravisham would dampen her interest in his affairs, and had every intention of relating the gist of their conversation to Adrianna before some chance remark made within her hearing should be misunderstood.

Adrianna was not without a few resolves of her

own. Looking her best in yellow muslin, she entered the drawing room slightly late for luncheon and found the Earl leaning against the mantelshelf, his handsome head bent in courteous attention to his aunts. Auntie F, the only one who was seated facing the door, saw her and rose. "Here you are at last," she said, moving forward. "Do let us repair to the dining room. I am certain Cook must be calling recriminations down upon your head."

By this time the Earl had pushed his shoulders away from the mantelshelf and crossed to Adrianna's side. "Cook will be advised to wait upon our pleasure," he remarked, holding out his arm.

Auntie A had a dreadful thought. "Adrianna, dearest, you took an unconscionable time in dressing. Whatever could you have been doing? Are you ill? No, I can see you aren't."

"Having asked and answered your own question, we presume you are now prepared to put away your needlework and join us at table," Auntie F remarked rather acidly.

The Earl, noting a stiffening of Auntie A's back, felt obliged to intervene. "Come, girls, do not let us bicker," he murmured, smiling tolerantly. "Remember that maintaining a placid mood cannot fail to aid one's digestion."

Applying the word "girls" in describing the elderly ladies took the trick, and they moved on to the dining room without further incident. Adrianna opted for her favorite seat at the Earl's right hand and brushed aside Auntie F's protest, saying that they would be more cozy gathered around one end of the long table. Auntie F was moved to say, "Informality has its place, Adrianna. We are prepared to accept laxity within the house, but I do hope you are not planning to make a habit of it when out-of-doors."

The Earl shot her a measuring glance. "I am sure that, when we set down to dinner, Adrianna is prepared to take her place at the foot of the table," he said.

Auntie A, with her disconcerting habit of catching a phrase and worrying it in her brain, said, "What do you mean, out-of-doors?"

"Ivor is teaching me to ride," Adrianna replied, taking the bit in her teeth.

"How considerate of him," Auntie A smiled.

"Astride," Adrianna added with resolution.

"Adrianna, dear!" Auntie C gasped, appalled.

Adrianna seemed determined to make a clean breast of it. "Wearing Ivor's outgrown breeches," she said, concluding her admissions.

His relations were momentarily bereft of speech. Even Auntie C could find nothing to say and stared at Adrianna in a bemused way. Auntie F found her tongue first, of course. "It appears my presence will lend countenance to your wife as well," she remarked to the Earl.

He frowned. "We will drop the subject," he said, annoyed that the conversation was taking place before the palpably interested butler and footman. "The fish was chosen with an eye to your preference. Kindly afford Jerves an opportunity to serve your plates."

The others, aware that Adrianna was gazing at him in lively astonishment, kept their eyes on their plates. "The turbot looks delicious," Auntie A remarked into the strained silence that followed. "Indeed I will have a portion, thank you, Jerves."

"Certainly, my lady," the footman bowed, his voice pregnant with suppressed curiosity. He would have liked to linger in the room after the serving was accomplished, but the Earl having dismissed him, he withdrew, his inquisitiveness unsatisfied.

"Servants have little enough to occupy their time," Auntie F observed when the door had closed behind him.

"They have scant contact with the outside world," Adrianna remarked. "It is no wonder we fascinate them so."

"Thank you, Adrianna, I had already realized that," Auntie F replied somewhat tartly.

The Earl sighed and embarked upon a discussion of a program for their entertainment designed to sooth ruffled feathers that lasted throughout the meal. He had just laid down his napkin at the conclusion of it when a disturbance was heard in the hall. Jerves soon came back into the dining room and said, with great dignity, "A groom from London, my lord, to see you on an urgent matter. I thought perhaps your lordship would wish him shown into your study."

The Earl's brows shot up. "Did he say what it is about?" he asked, surprised.

"Ravisham House had been burglarized, my lord."

"Thank you, Jerves. I will see him immediately," the Earl replied, rising.

"I will come with you," Adrianna said, jumping to her feet.

"No, I will see him alone, and then relate what he has to say. You have my word on it."

An hour later he went upstairs in search of her, knowing she would be waiting in her room. "Well, now," he chuckled, strolling in. "All agog, are you?"

"Don't be a beast!" she said, patting the seat on the sofa beside her. "Come over here, and tell me what he said."

"I don't know that he said anything of any particular importance," he commented, sitting down and leaning back at ease. "I like you in that dress, by the way."

"Must you be provoking?" she demanded, casting him a saucy look. "What happened in London?"

"I wish I knew. Boggs tells me someone did break into the house, but nothing seems to be missing."

"But that doesn't make sense. Why would anyone put himself to the trouble if he had no intention of stealing something? Are you pulling my leg?"

"Not at all. When I discover why he tore the paper from the backs of several paintings, and then rehung them, perhaps I will be able to answer that. Yes, I know, dear. It has a familiar ring."

"The Rubens, you mean."

"Grimcoe demonstrated an interest in it at

Twinfriars, you will recall. Leave the matter in my hands, Adrianna. I will engage to ascertain just what that interest entails."

"If you want to know what I think, he is looking for something concealed behind the canvas."

"Possibly."

"It could be jewelry," she pointed out.

"It could be many things, my dear, but I seriously doubt that gems would head the list."

"Why? Do you think you know what it is?"

"Let us say, rather, that I may have some idea of what it could be."

"That doesn't tell me very much. Ivor, I want to help. I could, you know. I have some very clever ideas at times."

"No," he said, not mincing matters.

"Well!" she said awfully. "I see now that there is a great deal to say for the belief that gentlemen reserve all the excitement for themselves."

"Not all of it," he grinned, reaching out an arm and pulling her against his side.

"Next you will tell me you plan to go to London without me."

"I'm afraid so," he admitted and kissed her.

"Somehow I thought you would say that. I would not need to leave the house."

"No, I will not take you with me, Adrianna. I plan to arrange for you to join me when I am sure it is safe."

She sighed and, knowing there was no way that she could change his mind, leaned her head against his shoulder. "Ivor," she murmured, "when I told your aunts about my breeches, why did

Auntie F say she would lend me countenance as well?"

"Did she say that?"

"You know very well she did."

"I am afraid I don't understand your question."

"Whom did she mean as well as? Was it you?"

"I sincerely trust not," he replied with a fine disregard for the truth.

Chapter 12

So the Earl journeyed to London accompanied only by his valet, while Adrianna remained at Ravisham and endured the daily monotony of entertaining the aunts. If her days seemed empty without his company, at least the visitors had no reason to complain. They were made to feel welcome, and if Adrianna sometimes wondered if they planned to stay on forever, she had no way of knowing that the Earl had requested they remain, at least until his return. He had, however, failed to reckon with Aunt Flournoy's wayward tongue. He had imposed silence on her, but she had come to hold Adrianna in the highest esteem and, from watching her pine for his return, found it impossible to stand silently by. The secret of Lady Palmer's interest in the Earl soon was out.

Auntie F descended the stairs one morning shortly after the arrival of the post to find Adrianna, who had been out riding attended by a groom, standing beside the table in the hall where the butler customarily placed the mail. The expression on her face left no doubt as to the contents of the letter she was in the process of perusing. "So Ravisham still has no plans for returning," Auntie F remarked, crossing the hall to peer over her shoulder at the letter.

Adrianna gave a start and thrust the sheets into a pocket of her breeches. "No—not as yet," she murmured, picking up her riding whip from the table where she had cast it, and turning away to go upstairs.

Auntie F sniffed. "It is not my intention to meddle," she said, while knowing full well she thoroughly intended to do just that, "but I never dreamed it could come to this."

"Come to what?" Adrianna asked, her interest caught.

"Men are all alike, drat them!"

"Are you speaking of Ivor?" Adrianna said, jerking her riding gloves between her fingers.

"I might have known he would be bound to be taken in by her!"

"Her?" Adrianna repeated with commendable steadiness.

"I have always despised a strumpet, whether she be high born or no. I warned him against her, but you may depend on it, he wouldn't listen. He never would. It was ever a flaw in the men of this family."

"Do you speak of Lady Palmer?" Adrianna asked in a tone that would have frozen a lady less impervious to a snub than Auntie F.

"We have no means of knowing the damage she has done," Auntie F replied. "Before I left London, she was running all about in search of Ravisham."

Adrianna looked shaken, but said, "You cannot know that he has been in her company. I appreciate your concern, really I do, but—no, I do not accuse Ivor of that."

Auntie F shook her head. "I have no wish to do the dear boy an injustice, but you will do well to defy him this once."

Adrianna could not help but laugh. "I am not in prison, Auntie F," she said.

"Then go to London yourself, where you can keep an eye on him. I am older and wiser than you, my dear. You will be advised to listen to me. But there, I will say no more. You will do as your conscience dictates, I know."

"You are being absurd," Adrianna replied. "If there is one thing I can be sure of, it is that Ivor would never countenance being spied upon. I daresay he would be furious."

"Let him!" Auntie F interpolated.

Adrianna ignored the outburst. "He is the soul of discretion," she continued. "He would never be guilty of doing anything that he would hesitate to relate to me. You may be very sure of that!"

The soul of discretion, at that precise moment, was being admitted into a house in South Lane Street. Following in the footman's wake, he walked up the stairs to the sitting room overlooking the street, where Lady Palmer awaited him dressed in a negligee of silk and lace. "Well, Lila," he said, raising a brow at her attire. "I am flattered you wished to see me, of course, but I will admit to some surprise. I hadn't expected to hear from you."

"It is not what you seem to think," she murmured, pulling the two sides of the garment closer together across her breasts. "Pour yourself a glass of wine. I sent out for a bottle of your favorite Madeira."

A gleam of amusement came into his eyes, but he picked up the decanter and poured out a glass. "You do not drink it, as I recall," he remarked, moving to a deep chair with an ottoman pulled up before it. "And now, Lila, may I ask why you have summoned me so urgently? I apprehend it is a matter of some importance, since it sent you looking all over town for me."

"How on earth did you know that?" she asked, startled.

"I seem to fall heir to all sorts of interesting information. Do you doubt it?"

"I had to send you a note, Ivor. When I could not seem to locate you, I didn't know what else to do."

He smiled. "Let us be honest with one another, Lila. If I had not received your missive, I would not be here now."

"I know," she replied, crossing one slender leg over the other. "Tell me, Ivor. Do you ever think of me?"

"If I said I didn't, you would be insulted," he replied with a diplomacy born of practice.

She smiled somewhat ruefully. "Ever the gentlemen," she said. "Your wife is indeed fortunate. Something tells me you will never play her false."

"I am glad to see you so creditably established," he remarked, turning the subject.

She shrugged, entirely cognizant of his ploy. "At least I am not out in the street," she said. "That ignominy has yet to befall me."

His brows rose. "Have you failed to secure a protector?" he said, studying her from under drooping lids.

She glanced at him, but fleetingly. "He is rather old, but I can't complain. You will say I could have done better for myself, I suppose."

"When was I ever rude?" he objected mildly.

A pang of yearning seized her. How many times in the past had he spoken just so? Taking herself in hand, she said, striving to make her voice light, "I did have a very good reason for sending for you, Ivor. Before I attracted the notice of the gentleman who—who assists me with my expenses, I had occasion to become acquainted with Viscount Shirley. You know him, I apprehend?"

"I do," said the Earl, taking snuff.

"Oh, Ivor!" she moaned. "I felt so old! He is so young!"

"He is well past the age of consent, my dear."

She sighed. "Yes," she admitted. "But he should never drink. Wine goes to his head. He is such a baby."

"Do not say he sniveled!" the Earl said, startled.

"No, he babbled," she replied half mournfully, half mirthfully. "At least it seemed so to me. His is not at all your smooth-spoken way, but then, not many men resemble you in that respect."

"What in the world are you talking about?" he inquired, putting his feet up on the ottoman.

"I am saying that you do not babble like other men."

"I certainly appreciate the esteem with which you regard my tongue, but what has that to do with my being here today?"

"Everything. Nothing. I don't know."

"You are extremely obliging, my dear, but where's the point of all this?"

"But I'm telling you!" she said. "Viscount Shirley made scant sense, but I did manage to unravel something of his ramblings. Am I correct in thinking that you know Lord Belderbrock?"

"Slightly," he murmured, his eyes steadily on her face.

"From what Shirley said, I should think it would be somewhat more than slightly."

"Mine has not been that honor," he remarked dryly. "Pray continue."

"It seems that Lord Belderbrock somehow attached himself to the Viscount's party while they were in attendance at a sporting event—a dog race, as I recall. Yes, I am certain it must have been. Shirley remarked on dropping a month's allowance on some nag."

"Not dogs," the Earl corrected. "Horses."

"That may be, but it is still a stupid way to lose one's money."

"I quite agree."

"Lord Belderbrock did not seem to mind. From what he told Viscount Shirley, he has expectations of coming into a great deal of cash."

"Indeed?" the Earl said, twisting the stem of his wine glass between finger and thumb, his eyes on the white liquid swirling in the glass. "You begin to interest me profoundly. From whom does Belderbrock expect to receive it?"

"From you, apparently."

The Earl was in the act of raising the wine glass to his lips, but paused with it suspended in mid-air. "How odd," he remarked, an inflection of surprise in his voice.

"Shirley thought so too," she agreed. "I haven't a notion why."

"I can give you any number of reasons 'why,' but none whatever for 'why not.' In fact, I have little doubt that Belderbrock is of the same mind where I'm concerned."

"Then why should he expect you to finance his excesses?"

"That," said the Earl, "is what Shirley is about to tell me. Helpful chap, the Viscount."

"And if he refuses?"

The Earl did not immediately reply to this, but sat gazing into space with a strange look upon his face. "He will, if I must choke it out of him," he said finally.

The immediate effect of this pronouncement was to send the Earl to the Viscount's lodgings in Pall Mall. Upon being informed by the porter that his lordship was in attendance at a prize fight some ten miles out of town, the Earl very sensibly strolled around to his club to partake of luncheon. From there he went to Jackson's Saloon and spent a pleasant hour working off his spleen sparring with the great Jackson himself. Dinner at Clarence House, followed by a visit to Almack's in the Regent's party, concluded the day. Returning home to Grosvenor Square at an unusually early hour, he told the hall porter that he might go to bed, and went on down the hall to his study. Except for the moonlight streaming into the open window, the room was in darkness. Some of the boredom left his face as he gazed out the window at the gardens in the back of the house. The air was alive with night sounds and the scent of roses. On an impulse, he stepped across the low windowsill and strolled among the flower beds to a path between rows of carefully trimmed, high hedges. Sitting down upon a stone seat, he breathed deeply of the sweet-smelling air and let his thoughts drift to Adrianna. At last sighing, he rose and returned to the house.

Stepping back inside, he had closed and bolted the window and turned away to go upstairs before he became undefinably aware that he was not alone in the room. Hard on the thought of a housebreaker came the conviction that Grimcoe had again gained entrance into the house. It had become obvious that Lord Charles's letters had been hidden behind one of the paintings found at Twinfriars, though by whom the Earl did not know. Not by Grimcoe certainly; he appeared to have scant idea where to search.

The moonlight cast dark shadows in the room, and it seemed to him that one of them seemed denser than the others. Treading silently, he moved swiftly forward and flung his arms around the intruder, dragging his quarry out of hiding without slackening the bear-hug he had around his victim. No housebreaker met his astonished gaze. "Adrianna!" he gasped, gazing down into her frightened face.

"Thank God!" she breathed in relief. "I thought you were a burglar! Why in the name of heaven did you come in through the window?"

"I went out through it. What are you doing here?"

"I couldn't sleep, and came down in search of something to read."

"Don't equivocate. You were to remain at Ravisham Hall."

She hung her head. "You must think it odd, finding me here," she said.

"I do."

"I had a particular desire to be with you."

It occurred to him that, while she displayed a seeming regret at having gone against his wishes, in reality she felt no regret at all. Slightly miffed, he said, "It could have been a burglar entering through the window. It was only by the luckiest chance that it wasn't. I should send you back to the country."

"But you won't," she murmured, gazing at him in some trepidation. "Will you?"

"No," he admitted, ruefully amused.

Smiling, she sank down into a chair. "What have you learned of the burglary?" she said, folding her hands together in a way that showed she was not prepared to budge.

Chuckling, he took a seat facing hers. "Very little," he said. "All of the paintings we brought from Twinfriars had been tampered with; in justice to the burglar, I must admit they sustained no damage."

"Indeed it was very bad of him, but he will know not to burgle here in future."

"If he burgles here again, my dear, he won't have a future."

"No, of course not," she gurgled. "Trust you to preserve your consequence."

"Very true," he replied, laughing. "I trust you realize I have it in my power to compel you to do as I wish."

"To make a cake of myself, you mean. Very well, sir. I will admit that I have behaved abominably. I should have sent word I was coming. There is no telling what mischief you will be obliged to hide."

"There is a saying that every good duelist

knows," he remarked, rising to take her hands in his and to pull her up into his arms. "Never underestimate the skill of your opponent."

"No, I mustn't, must I?" she murmured, subsiding in a very weak way against his chest and raising her face for his kiss.

"Ivor—" she began.

"Shhh!" he murmured, kissing her again.

"But—"

"Be quiet!" he ordered, sweeping her off her feet and walking with her toward the stairs.

Quite cowed, she uttered a confused protest at being carried, to which he paid no heed at all, then made no further attempt to say anything more. When she did speak again, he had taken her into his bedroom and undressed her. "You cannot mean for me to sleep with nothing on," she admonished halfheartedly.

"My precious idiot," he replied, laying her down upon his bed.

"I have a nightgown in my room," she remarked. "You have no notion of what I paid for it."

"I know precisely what you paid for it," he grinned, shrugging out of his coat and tossing it across a chair.

She gave a chuckle. "It seems a shame to let such an expensive garment go to waste."

"Wear it in your old age," he advised, stripping off his shirt. "At the present you have nothing to hide."

She gave another chuckle. "Do but consider the

sensibilities of your valet," she said. "Whatever will he think?"

"If he had any sensibilities at all, he would have left my service long ago," he countered. "And besides, he will not come until I ring the bell."

She watched him peel off his breeches, and abandoned any further attempt to bring him to a sense of the impropriety of his conduct. When he came to the bed, he stood for a moment gazing down at her before lying down beside her and taking her in his arms. "It's been hell to be away from you," he murmured, his warm hands on her in a way that made her tremble.

His mouth found hers and he kissed her hungrily, pressed kisses on her face and throat, moved on down to the soft curve of her breasts. "Love, my little love," he whispered, his hands stroking over and over her, cupping her breasts and teasing the nipples, on and on until she was quivering with pleasure at his touch. He came to her finally, the intensity of his passion spurring her on, until wildly, frantically, she moved with him and cried out with it, and collapsed limply in his arms when it was over.

"Now will you tell me that you missed me?" he murmured, bending over her to lovingly smooth the hair from her brow.

"Oh!" she said foolishly. "I was afraid you might not wish to return to my bed."

"Were you indeed?" he grinned, his hand going

157

to a breast. "And did you come chasing after me to make sure I did? Silly girl! I have been of a mind to send for you almost from the moment of first leaving you."

"You have?" she said, shaken with remorse. "But how dreadful of me. I had been imagining you in Lady Palmer's arms."

"Good God!" he said, astonished. "Wherever did you get that idea?"

"Auntie F said you would be bound to fall victim to her charms."

"The devil fly away with Auntie F. What else did she say?"

"Well, she said I should keep an eye on you, but I told her I knew you will tell me everything you have done."

"Not everything," he chuckled, the devil in his smiling eyes. "I am sorry your mind was put in a horrid dither, but I can assure you I did not fall victim to any female's wiles. Did you think I would?"

"No, why should I? I was used, before we were married, to think you a shocking profligate, although I did not quite understand what that meant at the time. But it has since occurred to me that you couldn't have been, not really. You have stayed by my side, have you not?"

"Yes," he agreed gravely. "I have."

"Well, then! That proves your morals are quite as good as mine!"

"I wouldn't go so far as to say that," he murmured, amused.

"Are you laughing at me?" she demanded, thrusting out her lip.

"My precious, I have some shocking news for you," he said. "I am a profligate. Let me catch my breath, and I will leave you in little doubt of that!"

Chapter 13

Adrianna set forth in the open barouche the following afternoon to visit a shop in Bond Street where she felt assured of being able to find ribbon to match an unusual shade of green gauze. The street was crowded with carriages disgorging smartly dressed ladies into the shops, and gentlemen strolling along the walks. Just as she came abreast of the entrance to Jackson's Boxing Saloon, she saw the Earl coming out. Waving to him, she told the coachman to stop, and eagerly leaned forward, watching him pick his way among the throng to the side of the barouche. "Where are you bound?" she asked. "May I take you up?"

"I will be glad of a ride to the bottom of the street," he smiled, getting into the carriage. "I am on my way to White's."

She looked at him rather curiously. "What do you do in your club all afternoon?" she asked.

"What do you do in the shops all day?" he countered.

"Spend your money," she gurgled. "You have not the least desire for me to become a dowd. Confess that you haven't."

His eyes swept over her. "May I say I cannot imagine any lady who could look less like a dowd?" he murmured obligingly.

She twinkled at him. "May I say I cannot imagine any gentleman who dresses so well as you?" she said. "And that, I believe, makes us even."

"Not quite," he said. "You have not the smallest desire to have me about the house all day."

"Try me," she returned, a complaisant expression on her face.

Smiling, he turned to direct the coachman to set him down at the next corner. The carriage turned onto Piccadilly and stopped. "Don't forget, we are engaged for tonight," he said, carrying her fingers to his lips. "Wear the silver satin. I particularly like you in it."

"Yes, I will," she replied as he stepped to the ground. "Don't be late in returning home."

He returned no answer to this parting sally, but merely stepped back and waved the coachman onward. Having winked at Adrianna as the carriage moved away, he strolled along Piccadilly to St. James's Street and on to White's. Surprised and delighted to perceive Viscount Shirley upon his entry into one of the rooms, he made his leisurely way to the arrangement of chairs where the Viscount was perusing the journals. "If you can spare the time, Shirley, I would like a word with you," he remarked, sitting down.

The Viscount laid aside the *Morning Chronicle* and said, "I had no idea you were in town, Ravisham. You cannot know how relieved I am to see you. I hadn't quite known just what to do, short of interrupting your honeymoon."

The Earl brushed aside this remark, saying, "A conversation I had with Lady Palmer left me consumed with curiosity. I understand you enjoyed an enlightening time with Lord Belderbrock."

"That is one way of putting it, certainly. He was drunk, you know. Drunk as a wheelbarrow."

"How distressing for you," the Earl murmured in heartfelt sympathy. "But continue, dear boy, pray continue."

"It was a disgraceful performance from start to finish," Viscount Shirley confided. "Entirely reprehensible. His lordship had the felicity—not shared by me, I might add—of attaching himself to a party of my friends at a—at a—"

"Horse race. I quite understand."

"Well, my papa wouldn't. One would almost suppose me in the habit of dropping sizable sums on the nags, to hear him tell it."

"My father was the same," the Earl said reassuringly. "I often found his lectures singularly unnerving. But back to the matter at hand. Lady Palmer seemed to think that Lord Belderbrock expects me to frank his losses."

"I'm dashed if I can make head or tail of it,

but he does expect it. He's a damned loose-screw, if you want my opinion."

"I quite agree," said the Earl.

"He was rather smug about it, I thought."

"No doubt he was, but do attempt to enlighten me further, Shirley. Did he say why he expects it?"

"Lord, I don't know. It had something to do with an estate you inherited, as best I could make out."

"Twinfriars?"

"Yes, so it was. I do remember that he mentioned that some connection he had with the place should prove extremely profitable to him."

"Do pardon my stupidity, Shirley," the Earl said, "but I don't follow you."

"Well, it stands to reason, Ravisham. I venture to say he spoke of 'his lordship' at least half a dozen times."

"I see," said the Earl. "Bear with me, Shirley, but did he by any chance give a name to this lordship?"

The Viscount shook his head. "Could he have meant someone other than yourself?" he asked after a moment.

"I am sure he did. There is food for speculation there, but I will appreciate it if you will not make anyone else privy to the thought."

"You can count on me, you know. My lips are sealed."

"Good!" the Earl said. "Shall we agree that I will be allowed to manage the affair in my own way from here on out?"

"So far as I'm concerned, you can, and welcome."

"Thank you, Shirley. I stand deeply in your debt. Are you for Vauxhall Gardens tonight? Fine. Do plan to join my wife and myself for dinner. You know our box."

"Is it to be a congenial party?" the Viscount asked, grinning.

"The best," the Earl laughed. "Belderbrock will not become a part of it."

Having gleaned all the information that Viscount Shirley had to impart, the Earl excused himself and shortly afterward strolled home to Grosvenor Square. My lady, he was informed upon inquiry of the butler, had not as yet returned to the house. Not in the least surprised, his lordship went on across the hall toward the stairs, a faint smile upon his lips. He was checked with his foot upon the first step by Mr. Longworth appearing in the library door. "My lord, if you have a moment?" the secretary began in hopeful accents.

The Earl smiled disarmingly. "Whatever it is, Edward, attend to it," he said. "I am sure you have no need of me."

"But, sir, I cannot attend to it," Mr. Longworth objected, holding out a missive written on soiled but curiously unwrinkled paper. "It arrived in this morning's post."

The Earl's brows rose. "Are you intending I touch that?" he asked, eyeing the letter askance.

"Simpson disinfected it, sir," Mr. Longworth explained.

His lordship looked surprised. "He appears to be a butler beyond price," he remarked. "May I inquire how he did so?"

A smile twitched at the corners of the secretary's lips. "I understand he ironed it, my lord," he said.

At that the Earl, who had been maintaining a straight face, gave a shout of laughter. "What a trial Simpson must find us," he said. "What does the letter say?"

Mr. Longworth looked rather perturbed. "I really think you should read it, my lord," he found the courage to persist.

"Later, Edward, later," the Earl replied, turning away.

"Shall I file it, my lord?"

"Precisely," his lordship tossed over his shoulder, and went on up the steps.

It was past six o'clock before Adrianna arrived home and hurried upstairs to dress. The Earl, hearing her rush by his door, listened to her step vanish into her own room and crossed to open the safe in the wall beside his bed. Removing a black velvet box, he tucked it under his arm and strolled through the connecting door between their bedrooms. Adrianna, just stepping into her tub, heard his voice speaking to her maid and called out that she would not be above a minute. The Earl, having a very good idea of her notions of time, went into her sitting room and sat down to wait.

Somewhat to his surprise, within only some few minutes over half an hour, she appeared in the

164

doorway, a vision in the silver satin, with a curl falling enticingly forward over one bare shoulder. "I'm not late after all," she announced with a saucy smile. "I rushed."

"Very commendable," he remarked, his gaze sweeping over her.

"You are ready early yourself," she said, moving forward.

"I am sure Edward finds me a trial," he replied, rising at her approach. "He wanted to detain me on some matter of business, but I much preferred to be dressed and waiting for you."

"Why?" she said, whirling about in an excess of joy.

"Stop teasing and I will show you."

"Am I doing that?" she said, coming to a halt before him.

"You damn well know you are," he grinned, unfastening the catch of the velvet box. "As you see, I have something for you."

"Oh!" she gasped, craning her neck.

"Hold still!" he admonished, his fingers busy with the clasp of the necklace he was fastening about her throat. "Now give me your hand."

She held it out, and he clasped a bracelet about her wrist and slipped a ring on her finger. "Emeralds!" she breathed, lightly brushing the stones with the tips of her fingers. "Oh, Ivor!"

"I did have a present for you," he said, catching her hand and carrying it to his lips. "We have been married one month today."

"Good God!" she said. "What a singular coincidence!"

He seemed to pause, then said in his tranquil way, "Am I expected to let that remark pass?"

"Yes, for I purchased a gift for you this afternoon," she said. "Is that not remarkable?"

"It is indeed."

"The only thing is, Ivor, I haven't got it. It's a gold snuff box, and your initials are being put on."

"Then I will withhold my gratitude until you do have it. If you are ready, my love, I will order the carriage brought around."

Adrianna took one last peek at the emeralds glowing around her throat before going with him from the room. "I feel just like a princess in a fairy tale," she confided, slipping her hand into his.

The evening undoubtedly would have ended on the same pleasant note with which it began had not Lady Palmer gone to Vauxhall Gardens also. Worse, Lady Temple went with her. As Adrianna well knew, Lady Temple did not like her. Youth and beauty, and even wealth, were perfectly acceptable attributes. Unfortunately, since a tendency toward spiteful remarks had lately become a habit with her, living next door to a charming Toast who enjoyed the privilege of being married to Ravisham had become just about more than Lady Temple could tolerate. From having been unable to attach him for herself, a circumstance unknown to anyone other than the Earl himself, her resentment of Adrianna had grown until it assumed alarming proportions. She only needed the chance to bring down vengeance upon

Adrianna's unsuspecting head. The opportunity arose immediately following supper.

Adrianna had been enjoying herself hugely. The food had been excellent, the Earl attentive, the members of their party gay and admiring of her new jewelry. It was not until she encountered Lady Temple at the waterfall that it all went awry. Their entire party had left their box to stroll along the paths en route to view the cascade, but by the time they arrived at it, various among their number had wandered away to greet other friends, the Earl among them. Entranced by the steep fall of water, Adrianna stood gazing at it, rapt, until a voice at her shoulder interrupted her reverie.

"It cannot compare with the waterfall at Chatsworth," Lady Temple remarked. "But then, I am sure you know that."

Adrianna turned her head. "No, I did not know," she said, the gleam of amusement in her eyes the result of her ladyship's name-dropping.

Lady Temple found no trouble at all in reading the meaning behind those innocent-sounding words. "No doubt Ravisham will escort you to it when you visit there," she said, annoyed. "I understand he lost no time in showing it to Lila Palmer."

The barb struck home, as Lady Temple knew it would. "I am sure it is worthy of note," Adrianna remarked, determined not to display the hurt before her ladyship's expectant eyes.

"Do forgive me," Lady Temple murmured. "I hadn't thought that Ravisham and Lila would be bored by this pale imitation of Chatsworth. It seems they are. I wonder where they have got to, don't you?"

In spite of herself, Adrianna looked around. The Earl was nowhere in sight. "My husband strolled off with Viscount Shirley," she said, a slight quaver in her voice which she could not control.

"Oh?" Lady Temple murmured, a sweetly sympathetic smile curving her hateful lips. "But, of course. If you insist."

Adrianna could not help glaring. "Don't use that tone with me!" she said somewhat inadvisedly.

"Oh, my dear!" Lady Temple breathed soothingly. "I thought you knew. I am sure I would never let the cat out of the bag on purpose. I do hope I am wrong."

"If you will excuse me," Adrianna said, turning away.

"Yes, do go in search of him," Lady Temple called after her retreating back. "If he is alone, just ask him. He will deny being in Lila's company, of course, but it will set your mind at rest."

Adrianna, hurrying along a path to return to their box, rounded a corner and stopped dead in her tracks. Lady Palmer and the Earl were standing close together in the walk just ahead. White, shaken, dying inside, Adrianna whisked herself out of sight and fled before the Earl became aware of her presence. It was a great deal too bad. She missed seeing him bow politely to Lady Palmer, then turn on his heel and stride away. For the remainder of that fateful evening, Adrianna stayed determinedly cheerful. But once they entered their carriage to return home, her spirits seemed to flag. The Earl, putting it down to fatigue, leaned quietly back in his corner of the seat, respecting her silence.

It was a mistake. When he opened the connecting door between their bedrooms, he found her room in darkness. Pausing to allow his eyes to adjust, he could just make out the lump her body made curled up in the center of her bed. Smiling slightly, he removed his robe and sat down on the edge of her mattress. "You aren't asleep," he remarked, reaching for the covers to turn them back.

For answer, she jerked the quilts from his grasp and burrowed deeper beneath them.

His brows rose. "What the devil!" he ejaculated.

She gave an infuriated little flounce. "Go away!" she said coldly.

"Adrianna, you have been acting strangely since we left Vauxhall Gardens," he said. "What happened to make you like this?"

"As if you didn't know!" she muttered, her voice muffled by the covers.

"I don't," he said, tossing the quilts aside with a sudden movement that caught her unawares.

"No!" she gasped, sitting up to slip from the bed.

He was on her in an instant, his weight crushing her down into the pillows. "Don't fight me," he murmured, his mouth searching and finding hers in the dark. Her head held immobile by his hand buried in her hair, she fought to turn her head away, but could only struggle helplessly in his grasp, her protests smothered under his lips. "Why?" he demanded, raising his head to stare down at her.

"I saw you!" she flung at him. "You flaunt your mistress abroad, you—you—"

He drew a sharp breath. "How dare you!" he said furiously through his teeth. "Your mistrust of me passes all bounds!"

Her eyes flashed. "How dare I?" she exclaimed. "How dare you, sir! Well, you can just go away. You shan't come to me fresh from another woman's arms!"

"Adrianna," the Earl began grimly, "I won't remind you that you are my wife, for you are well aware of it. It will, however, give you a notice that will not come amiss. I will come to your bed when I choose, and as often as I choose, and by God, ma'am, you will welcome me, or it will be very much the worse for you!"

She heard him out in silence, white with anger. "Oh, will I?" she said. "Well, sir, I have no intention of swelling the ranks of your conquests! You shan't make love to me in between your—your harlots and—and—opera dancers!"

"A woman of taste and refinement would not speak of such!" he shot back, perilously close to completely losing control of his temper. "The manners obtaining in the wilds of Sussex will not serve in the confines of our home. You will submit, as a dutiful wife should, or I will use you as I would use the harlot you are so fond of mentioning!"

"Oh!" she stormed. You may be certain of this, my lord: I don't love you, and I won't submit! Never in a million years!"

"You have now given full rein to your tongue," he spat, by now quite as furious as she. "Well, I warned you that I will use you as you deserve."

"Don't you dare! No! Oh!" she wailed as his mouth parted her lips.

Affected more by the contact than she would admit, even to herself, she struggled desperately to free herself, but her strength was no match for his. He had one arm about her shoulders, and a leg across her body, making it impossible for her to move. His free hand stroked her breasts and thighs, his fingers probing with a sure knowledge of her tender parts that left her blushing in the dark. Her hands pushed futilely against his shoulders, but she could not budge him. She did protest weakly when his lips left hers and moved down to her breasts, but her treacherous body was responding to his in a way that it had not done before. She could not believe that the hoarse voice speaking to him belonged to her, nor that the body rising to meet his and striving for fulfillment belonged to her. And then when the convulsive trembling seized her, she could only moan and clutch his shoulders and sob out her release with her face buried in his throat.

The Earl, his passion spent, put her from him and sat up. "You may not love me, madam," he said in a voice that froze her to the marrow, "but I warned you I will compel your will."

She found that she was trembling, his words

stabbing her to the quick. "You beast!" she cried. "I almost hate you!"

His nostrils flared. "You leave me no doubt of that!" he said sardonically. "Console yourself with the reflection that I did not hurt you as I could have done."

"How noble of you!" she shot back, just as sarcastic.

He rose. "The next time I come to your bed, I will expect your willingness without protest," he said and stalked from the room, leaving her gasping.

Upon reflection, she knew herself more at fault than he. There could be no defending her spiteful words. Why, oh why, had she told him she did not love him, that she did, in fact, hate him? It was small wonder he had not scrupled to humiliate her, nor to use her as he had. She had goaded him into it, there was no blinking that. His own conduct, on the other hand, had been unpardonable, there was no denying that. All the joy of their marriage was at an end, utterly destroyed. She could not face him, could not live with his disgust. Such agitated thoughts brought a lump in her throat. She would go away. She had no choice. And perhaps someday, when the wounds had had time to heal, he might want her back again.

Chapter 14

It was just upon the dusk when the Accommodation coach lumbered into the courtyard before the inn and drew to a lurching stop before the door. The steps were let down and several passengers descended to the ground, Adrianna among them. By no stretch of the imagination could she be said to resemble the usual patron of a stagecoach. A velvet pelisse edged in sable, a muff of the same fur, and a very fashionable bonnet proclaimed her station. The coachman, finding himself in a quandary, hitched up his reins and clambered down from the box to extricate her valise from the boot with his own hands, an unprecedented action on his part. He further surprised himself by asking if he could be of service and, upon being informed that she required a carriage, rolled into the inn in search of the landlord. It soon developed that a carriage was out of the question. Would my lady condescend to a gig? She would. The stage had been crowded, and the journey a most uncomfortable one.

The conveyance, when brought around, was seen to be a rickety one with a hard seat, pulled by a horse only slightly less ancient than the light, two-wheeled, open carriage. Most happily for Adrianna, the evening was not likely to come on to rain. She stepped up into the gig, moved over to make room on the seat beside her for her valise, and leaned back with a sigh, relieved not to have been overtaken by the Earl. It had been with no high hopes that she boarded the Accommodation coach in London earlier in the day. Had any other choice offered, she would not have done so. But no other choice had offered. Had she sought more agreeable transportation, the Earl would have discovered her whereabouts in a trice. Once the door of Twinfriars closed behind her, she would not so easily be dislodged.

She was recalled to a sense of her surroundings by the horse's slackening pace and turning into a private road. It needed no daylight for her to know herself on Twinfriars' ill-kept carriage-way. The gig bounced along over the uneven ground for several hundred yards, then drew to a standstill before the rambling house. Seen in the moonlight, it still had the power to appall her. She would not have been at all surprised had Chittering opened the door, as taciturn as ever. It was, however, a young footman in impeccable livery who answered her ring. She scarcely noticed him, for her attention was claimed by the change in the house, which was sufficiently startling to cause her to check on the threshold and to look about her with a great deal of astonishment.

The rooms shone. There could be no other way to describe it. Candlelight glittered on sparkling crystal and shimmered on the polished surfaces of furniture and floors. The walls were freshly papered, the woodwork painted pristine white. Worn upholstery had been replaced, as had the drapery and rugs. Everywhere she looked, the grandeur of the past had been restored. Her bemused gaze alighted presently upon the servant who had admitted her. "I am the Countess of Ravisham," she said, smiling. "Is Mrs. Chittering in the house?"

To his credit, he masked his surprise. "She is, my lady," he said, bowing. "Shall your ladyship wish her to immediately wait upon you?"

"In the drawing room, please. Desire someone to kindle the fire, if you will, and order tea sent in to me. What is your name, by the way?"

"It is Pervis, my lady."

"Well, Pervis, I am glad to have you in my employ. Have my valise taken to my rooms. I suppose it is too much to hope that a personal maid has been engaged to serve me?"

"Her name is Francel, my lady."

"Never say she is French?" she said, startled.

"I understand that she is, my lady. His lordship engaged her services at the same time he engaged mine. We came down from London together."

"Very well, Pervis. That will be all for now," she said and went into the drawing room. She was indeed pleased with the salon. The walls above the wainscot were hung with a delicate green paper, and the drapery at the tall windows was of green and cream silk tied back with cords to which were attached long silken tassels. A Savonerie carpet in green and cream and rose covered the floor and supported sofas and chairs upholstered in brocade. English Sheraton satin-wood tables, a pair of Venetian consoles surmounted by mirrors, a French girandole, and a handsome viz-a-viz imparted a cosmopolitan flavor to the room. The entire effect was eclectic and utterly charming. She was just wondering how the Earl had found time to see to it all when a rap sounded on the door and Mrs. Chittering came hurrying in.

"'Tis glad I am to see you, my lady," she beamed, bustling forward. "We just this week finished putting the house to rights, though your ladyship may have noticed there is still much to do outside."

"You have worked wonders," Adrianna assured her, smiling. "I shouldn't have thought it possible."

"His lordship sent workmen down from London to hasten things along. I will say this for them, my lady. They may have been underfoot, but they did know their trade. His lordship should be best pleased, when all's said."

"I am sure he will," Adrianna said feebly.

"When the late Master took and died, there was scarce a servant left on the place, but his lordship's secretary took care of that. I think your ladyship will find we can look after you in prime style."

This proved to be the case. Within a surprisingly short space of time, a fire burned on the hearth and a tea of scones and jam had been brought in. Adrianna sat down at the table and poured herself a cup. Mrs. Chittering, having volunteered to show her over the house the following morning, and having had the offer accepted, bustled off to the kitchens on some half-expressed errand of her own, leaving Adrianna to enjoy her tea in peace. The period of quiet reflection helped to soothe her agitated spirits. Since she had left Ravisham House that morning, she had been forced to fend for herself as best she might. It was pleasant to find a staff of servants at Twinfriars waiting to smooth the way for her.

She was about to ascend the stairs to her bedchamber when she recalled that Grimcoe had somehow gained entrance during her previous stay in the house. Knowing that she could not go to bed with any degree of assurance until she discovered if a secret entrance had been found and sealed, she turned back and went to the kitchens in search of Mrs. Chittering. Both the Chitterings were there, much to Adrianna's surprise. It was soon explained. Chittering had been—as she had guessed—the head groom in his late lordship's stables, a post his lordship the Earl had permitted him to retain. Adrianna thought it wise to accept the Earl's judgment, in the circumstances. Raising objections might well reveal her presence at Twinfriars, and Chittering could just turn out to be a top-flight groom. Told by him that the house had been zealously searched with "nowt of a secret passage" come to light she went up to bed still feeling some unease, Chittering's assurance notwithstanding. Resolved to resume the search herself, she fell asleep at last and slept undisturbed until morning.

As things turned out, it was Pervis who joined in the search, Chittering having given it as his considered opinion that she was wasting her time. Still young enough to look upon the whole affair as a diversion and something of a lark, Pervis went about the house inspecting the walls for sliding panels and tapping them in high hopes of hearing a hollow sound. Adrianna accompanied him more from an appreciation of the ridiculous than from any real expectations of her own. She hadn't the heart to suggest that, were there any openings in the walls, the painters and paper hangers would surely have come across them. The walls disposed of, the floors became the focal point of young Pervis's attention. Alas, an hour spent in tugging the furniture and rugs about failed to disclose so much as one trap door, inspect the floor boards as closely as he might. Disappointed, he begged pardon for having been unsuccessful in his endeavors and asked if he could be of further service.

"It is a great deal too bad that we couldn't find it," Adrianna said. "I am convinced the intruder gained entry by some means other than a door or window. Since I have not the least desire that he should repeat the performance, we will continue the search another time."

"I shouldn't think he will return, my lady, now that the staff has been enlarged," Pervis replied, emboldened.

"That did not deter him from breaking into Ravisham House in London," Adrianna said. "No, I am convinced that since he failed to find what he was looking for there, it must be here."

"May I inquire why your ladyship feels that it is?"

"The dust covers behind some paintings originally located here had been removed. I thought perhaps jewelry had been concealed there, but the Earl did not seem to think so. I wonder what it could have been."

"I should think papers of some sort, my lady."

Adrianna stared at him, much struck. "I do believe you may be right," she said thoughtfully. "His late lordship preferred to invest in art. He would have had no interest in papers of any sort. I am beginning to believe someone had taken advantage of his illness to further his own ends."

"That could account for the intruder, my lady. His being surprised here after his late lordship's death would indicate he had not had an earlier opportunity to remove the papers. I understand his lordship spent his final days in isolation."

"I daresay that is it, Pervis. Well, that certainly narrows the field. At least we know what to look for. Mrs. Chittering knows the house as well as anyone. I will consult with her."

The housekeeper, however, had nothing to offer

when Adrianna sent for her later in the day. The lawyers had turned over all of his late lordship's papers to his heir, the Earl. Nothing could have exceeded Mrs. Chittering's confidence that Twin-friars sheltered little of any real value. "I fancy the late Master spent every shilling he could lay his hands on for those pictures he set such store by. Not to mention the heathenish idols he kept in his rooms," she added, sniffing disdainfully.

Passing over this derogatory reference to the exquisite jades and ivories, Adrianna remained entirely unconvinced. "I mean to be prepared," she said. "The intruder may return. I haven't as yet had an opportunity to discover if there is a weapon in the house."

Mrs. Chittering's eyes grew round. "My lady!" she gasped. "Never say you mean a pistol!"

"If there is one. If there isn't, I noticed a pair of crossed swords on the wall in the main hall."

Mrs. Chittering allowed her disapproval to show on her face. "If I may say so, my lady, if you are set on confronting a vicious criminal, Mr. Chittering should keep watch outside your door."

This, however, Adrianna would by no means agree to, saying instead that she would set Pervis to patrolling the halls. Mrs. Chittering next suggested that she bear her ladyship company throughout the night, an offer Adrianna hastened to refuse. "I do not imagine I shall be in any real danger," she explained. "I only want to discover the hiding place of—whatever it is that has been hidden here. If he knows himself, that is."

Mrs. Chittering set scant store by Pervis's ability to protect his mistress, but nevertheless went away to inform him of his new responsibility. Adrianna herself put scant reliance on his experience in dealing with persons of the lowest orders, but when it came to a choice between Chittering and Pervis, it would have to be Pervis.

Protection in any form proved to be unnecessary. It had been long before she slept, but the hours passed without incident. Pervis, who shortly after nine o'clock she found standing guard outside her door, seemed to be little tired for having been awake throughout the night. It was plain he viewed the chance of catching an intruder as great sport. Adrianna declined to enter into a speculation as to what might occur during the coming night and, having sent him off to bed, went on downstairs to partake of breakfast.

Chapter 15

At about the time Adrianna was descending the stairs at Twinfriars in Sussex, the Earl had that instant come in and was crossing the hall at Ravisham House in London. It was evident he had been riding, for he wore top-boots and buckskin breeches and a plain but expertly tailored coat of brown cloth. He too had experienced difficulty in falling asleep the previous night, but for a different reason. He had not been long out of her presence before he bitterly regretted his conduct. It had been anything rather than that of a model for excellence, and he knew it. From losing his temper, he had spoiled everything. He should have discovered the reason for her distress. The impropriety of her behavior was nothing when compared with the want of delicacy he himself had shown. It was not enough to say he had been provoked into actions which were ill-judged.

For womanlike, Adrianna, when wounded, had merely given utterance to the most stabbing phrases she could bring to her tongue.

So sunk in foolish pride had he become that he had allowed the following day to pass without making amends. Nor had he seen anything of her during those same interminable hours. He had spent a miserable second night apart from her, disturbed by unquiet dreams until, by the time the first light began to filter in through the curtains, he was glad to leave his solitary bed. A considerable portion of his early morning ride had been spent in considering in just what phrases he would couch his apology, and in selecting just what words he would employ in making his declaration of love. With this uppermost in his mind, he had returned to the house by eight o'clock thoroughly intending to go straight upstairs to her room, only to be gainsaid in this, however, by the butler's informing him that Lord Charles had come to call.

"At this hour of the morning?" the Earl said, raising his brows.

"I have shown his lordship into the breakfast room," Simpson explained, relieving the Earl of his curly-brimmed beaver hat.

"Oh?" the Earl murmured, handing him his whip and gloves. "I will join him immediately. Thank you, Simpson."

"By a fortunate circumstance, my lord," Simpson continued while accepting the whip and gloves, "Cook has arisen in a complaisant mood this morning."

This thinly veiled disapproval of an early morning caller demanding breakfast brought a slight smile to the Earl's lips. "Kindly discover if Cook's complaisance extends so far as to encompass breakfast for me," he said, going in his leisurely way down the hall to join his friend.

Lord Charles looked up from the dish of bacon and eggs before him, a twinkle in his eye. "Damn, but I'm glad to see you," he grinned, stabbing with his fork in the general direction of the Earl. "That man of yours don't approve of feeding me, you know."

"Dear me," the Earl said, his eyes brimful with amusement.

"Thought he'd go into an apoplexy before my very eyes."

"You appall me," the Earl replied, strolling forward.

"Gave me to understand you aren't home to callers before the hour of eleven, as a rule. I didn't dare ask for ale."

"Worse and worse. Accept my condolences," the Earl said, crossing to the bell and pulling it. "You are up and about early for you, Jaimie."

"I know it's a devilish early hour, but it can't be helped," Lord Charles replied plaintively. "This isn't a courtesy call."

"At eight o'clock in the morning, I should hope not," the Earl remarked somewhat pointedly.

This hint passed completely over Lord Charles's head. "It's m'tiger," he mumbled around a mouthful of food. "Plague take the brat!"

"Now, don't tell me that Lord Chester has

finally succeeded in—er, luring him away from you," the Earl begged, crossing to take his seat at the table. "It sounds rather like it, dear boy. What else would have sent you abroad upon the world without your breakfast?"

"Well, it's not my fault I'm not at my best before noon, you know. Besides, it ain't that!"

The butler just then ushered in a footman bearing the Earl's breakfast on a tray, temporarily putting a stop to further conversation. "Beg pardon, my lord," he said. "Did you ring?"

"I did," the Earl replied. "Have the goodness to send in a pitcher of ale for his lordship."

"Very good, my lord," Simpson replied. "Will your lordship wish Viscount Shirley shown into the small salon?" he added after an infinitesimal pause.

"Shirley!" the Earl ejaculated, looking surprised.

"His lordship has just this moment arrived," Simpson explained, his face a masterpiece of detached disinterest.

"Show the Viscount to this room," the Earl said, glancing at Lord Charles. "I imagine you are as surprised as I," he added, pouring himself a cup of coffee.

"Well, I am glad that you recognize that," Lord Charles grinned. "It's all the same with me, dear boy, if the whole town takes it into its head to drop in for breakfast."

"I hope we will find you are mistaken in anticipating that," the Earl remarked, putting down the coffee pot. He had scarcely done so when the door opened and Viscount Shirley walked in, magnificently arrayed in full evening dress. "Dear me," he added, his amused gaze roaming over the new arrival. "You will not have eaten. May I offer you something?"

Viscount Shirley eyed the egg Lord Charles was conveying to his mouth, and shuddered. "My dear fellow, no," he said, dropping into a chair.

"Deuced queer hours you keep, if you don't mind my saying so," Lord Charles remarked, eating the egg.

"Well, you're here, if you don't mind my saying so," the Viscount pointed out, though somewhat stiffly.

"But I am here on a matter of business," Lord Charles explained vaguely.

"So am I," the Viscount snapped. "My business with Ravisham is private, I might add."

"What you want is some libation," Lord Charles grinned, motioning to Simpson, who had just come in with the pitcher of ale. "It does worlds for the digestion, you know."

"Ale!" Viscount Shirley uttered explosively.

"Don't you agree it's a capital notion for breakfast?" Lord Charles teased. "For myself, I never drink it either; not just before going to bed, that is."

The Earl put down his knife and fork. "Spare me your bickering," he said. "I fancy you are both here upon the same errand. Or am I laboring under some delusion?"

"Are we, by Jupiter!" Lord Charles said, staring.

"You have news to impart concerning Belderbrock," the Earl continued.

"How in thunder did you know that?" Lord Charles demanded, goggling.

"But, I'm omniscient, dear boy. I thought you knew."

"Well, if that don't beat all!"

"Quite," the Earl chuckled, turning to the Viscount. "You first, Shirley," he said. "I presume you spent some time last evening in Lady Palmer's company?"

The Viscount blinked. "Well, yes," he admitted. "But it wasn't what you think!"

"I think nothing at all," the Earl said with a lurking smile. "Pray say what you have come to say."

"Well, it was Lady Palmer who told me he had gone into Sussex—Belderbrock, I mean. You are right about that. Don't you own some property there?"

"My wife does. Twinfriars."

"Yes, that's the place. Well, Belderbrock told Lila he had some business to attend to there."

"At Twinfriars?" the Earl ejaculated, sitting bolt upright.

"He was drunk, you understand. He must have been, to think he would have contact with your wife."

"My wife!" the Earl blinked. "No, by Jove, he couldn't! Adrianna is safely asleep upstairs."

"I thought it sounded devilish like a hum, but Lila insisted you should be informed. What do you mean to do?"

"That depends somewhat on what Jaimie has to say."

"Eh?" Lord Charles gasped. "I know nothing of it. I'll tell you what, Ivor. That's a damnable thing to say!"

"Not Belderbrock going into Sussex, my good fool," the Earl protested, shaking his head. "What you came here to tell me."

"Oh, that," Lord Charles said sheepishly. "I put my tiger to following him, as you suggested. On the whole, I believe he enjoyed the assignment. At least he has not let Belderbrock out of his sight. To hear Ted tell it, his lordship frequents the oddest places, and in the most disreputable company you can imagine."

The Earl had become very still with this final remark. "Could this company have been a barrel-chested man, with long arms, a short neck, and somewhat garish taste in dress?" he murmured, his eyes never wavering from Lord Charles's face.

"What the devil!" Lord Charles gasped. "Do you know him?"

"I rather fancy I do."

"Damn if that don't beat all," Lord Charles said, staring.

"Yes, it does, rather, doesn't it," the Earl remarked, adding, "You said that Belderbrock frequents the oddest places?"

"Places, yes, Ivor. Also people. Young Ted trailed him to Lord Chester's address in Curzon Street. Now, what do you make of that?"

"Nothing, at the moment. Might I inquire if his

—er, odd companion accompanied him to Chester's house?"

"No, but Ted tells me Belderbrock went immediately from Curzon Street to a low haunt on the river front where it seems they met. Stormy was among the less colorful of the epithets Ted employed in describing Belderbrock's face. The whole thing is deuced queer, if you ask me."

"I cannot agree with that, Jaimie," the Earl said calmly. "It is a fortunate circumstance."

"It is nothing of the kind!" Lord Charles protested. "You know very well I cannot have Ted chasing all over town playing the sleuth while I go without his services!"

"But only think of the nest of thieves uncovered," the Earl remarked without a trace of emotion in his level voice.

"Good God!" Lord Charles gasped, the light dawning suddenly. "Lord Chester!"

"Quite."

"Well, if that don't beat all!"

Viscount Shirley gazed from one of them to the other. "If what doesn't beat all?" he asked, perplexed.

The Earl's attention became focused upon him. "Do you happen to know if a ruffian accompanied Belderbrock into Sussex?" he inquired.

"Now you mention it, I rather fancy that someone may have. At least Lila thought so. She said that Belderbrock spoke of taking a friend along to do the dirty work. Lila assumed he was speaking of a gardener, though she had no idea what he could want with one."

"I have been a blind fool," the Earl remarked, his mouth grim. "Of course they have gone to Twinfriars. The letters must still be hidden there."

"You mean—" Lord Charles prompted, staring.

"Precisely, my dear fellow," the Earl replied. "They have not found them because Uncle William must have come across them first."

Lord Charles grinned. "Then all we have to do is to find them ourselves," he said.

"Unless Uncle William destroyed them, yes. No, do not look too hopeful, Jaimie," he added, rising to ring the bell. "It would be more like him to have rehidden them for some purpose of his own. Nothing criminal, you understand, but Uncle William liked his jest."

"Well, I'll tell you this, Ivor: it is no joke to me."

The butler entered at this moment in answer to the summons with a promptness that indicated he had been lurking just outside the door. "You rang, my lord?" he said, waiting expectantly.

The Earl cast him a perfectly knowing glance and said, "I am going into Sussex for a few days, Simpson. Desire Upton to pack a valise for me."

"Very good, my lord. Might I inquire if Upton is to accompany you?"

"He will follow with my luggage. Oh, and Simpson, send someone around to Lord Charles's lodgings with instructions to pack for him."

"Really, old boy!" Lord Charles interjected.

"The phaeton will be out front in, say, one hour," the Earl continued, ignoring the outburst.

"Yes, my lord," Simpson replied. "May I inquire after your lordship's destination?"

"I am going to Twinfriars. Please discover of her ladyship's maid if her ladyship is awake."

"I will say this for you," Lord Charles remarked after the butler had withdrawn. "You waste no time, once you make up your mind."

"I wish someone would explain all this to me," Viscount Shirley asked of the room at large.

"It concerns a scoundrel, a fool, and a rip, but we won't go into it now," the Earl replied. "I would take you with me, Shirley, but I am not at liberty to divulge a confidence."

"You mean Jaimie here, I suppose," the Viscount grinned, an unholy gleam stealing into his eyes. "There is a lady mixed up in it somewhere, mark my words. I would not be unduly surprised to learn it is Lottie."

"Eh?" Lord Charles blinked. "What d'you know of Lottie?"

"Really, Jaimie, you should have kept the chit in better order," the Viscount chuckled. "She chastized you to Freddie Finklebine for being not only callous, but niggardly into the bargain. 'Pon my word, she did."

"I knew it!" Lord Charles exclaimed disgustedly. "Of all the—the—"

"Now, now, dear boy, don't get your wind up. She is currently under Freddie's protection, you know. He won't let her tattle, take my word for it."

The Earl and Lord Charles exchanged a thought-

191

ful look. "How well do you know this Lottie?" the Earl asked, correctly interpreting Lord Charles's brief nod.

The Viscount flushed. "Well enough," he said.

The Earl and Lord Charles exchanged a second look. Again Lord Charles gave an imperceptible nod of his head. Whereupon the Earl outlined a brief summary of events to date, ending with the request that the Viscount join them in their quest. "You are in a position to aid us immensely," he said. "It should be a simple matter for you to discover what she did with the letters."

"Yes, by Jove, I believe I could!" the Viscount enthused. "I doubt she sold them. She's not in funds, you know, but she's not one to stoop so low."

"When was she ever in funds?" Lord Charles snorted. "I'll tell you what, Ivor. She is not a bad sort. She may be an addlepate, but she ain't devious. Whoever got them from her did it on a ruse."

"I am sure he did," the Earl remarked. "Shirley, shall we expect you at Twinfriars in, say, three days? If you feel that will allow you sufficient time, that is."

Viscount Shirley looked startled. "No reason to think I can't make it by then, no reason at all," he said. "The thing is, it ain't above a half-day's drive."

"I refer to your—er, assignation with Lottie," the Earl explained.

"Lottie? Oh, yes, of course. No trouble there.

Shouldn't think that would take above a night."

"I trust your confidence is not misplaced," the Earl remarked with some humor.

"You mean Freddie, I apprehend."

"Something of the sort."

"Oh, Freddie won't mind. A great gun, is Freddie."

The Earl was saved the necessity of replying by the entrance of the butler. "Excuse me, my lord," he said, "but her ladyship seems not to be in the house."

A muscle twitched in the Earl's cheek. Recovering himself swiftly, he said, "May I inquire after her whereabouts?"

"Her ladyship's maid informs me her ladyship left for Twinfriars at an early hour on yesterday morning," Simpson replied, a slight quaver in his voice belying the schooled impassivity of his bearing.

"Yesterday morning!" the Earl gasped, reeling under the shock.

"Her ladyship confided to her maid that you approved of the journey, my lord," the butler explained, loathe to have the blame fall upon his own shoulders.

"Why was I not informed?" the Earl demanded.

Simpson's hand shook slightly. "No one saw fit to communicate the intelligence to me," he said.

A scowl came upon the Earl's face. "No doubt Coachman will see fit to impart the details to me," he snapped. "Send for him at once!"

"Certainly, my lord," Simpson bowed.

Something in his tone caught the Earl's attention. "You sound doubtful," he said.

"I understand her ladyship did not order the carriage, my lord."

"Oh? What did she order?"

"A hired hackney, my lord."

The Earl's eyes widened. "I begin to see daylight," he remarked. "I am sure the staff will be charmed to assist you in removing the entire household to Twinfriars."

Simpson's face fell. "Certainly, my lord," he said.

"You will leave a skeleton staff here to await our return."

Simpson brightened perceptibly. "Certainly, my lord," he repeated.

"You yourself will go to Twinfriars."

Simpson's face fell again. "Yes, my lord," he said.

"Further, you will instruct her ladyship's maid to pack her ladyship's entire wardrobe. Upton will pack my own."

"Your entire wardrobes. Yes, my lord."

"Also the household linens, the paintings, and my lady's writing desk."

"Yes, my lord," Simpson said dismally.

"A coach will be put at Cook's disposal for transporting foodstuffs sufficient for two week's stay."

Simpson forgot himself so far as to blink. "A coach, my lord, yes," he said with an effort.

"Further, Mr. Longworth will move his base of

operations to Twinfriars. That also is understood."

"Yes, my lord," Simpson replied, his face once again impassive.

"Good. I think we now understand one another. I trust the entire staff will do so shortly."

"I think I may safely promise that in future your lordship will be informed of all matters pertaining to the household," Simpson said from the heart.

"We do understand one another," the Earl remarked with the glimmer of a smile. "Very well, Simpson. You may go."

Lord Charles watched Simpson bow himself from the room, and grinned. "Damn if you aren't monstrous," he said.

"Do not distress yourself, Jaimie," the Earl replied. "No doubt the staff will find itself with sufficient cause to reorder its thinking."

"I can well believe it," Lord Charles chuckled. "By Gad, but you're a cool devil!"

"I have been called worse," the Earl remarked, still with the glimmer of a smile.

"What is want to know is," Lord Charles said, "why should a lady of your wife's standing elect to order a hackney carriage?"

"Do strive to cultivate a little imagination, Jaimie," the Earl replied. "It is perfectly understandable. Adrianna has quite plainly thrown down the gauntlet."

"Which you are picking up?"

"But, of course, dear boy. I merely follow her lead."

"Oh?" Lord Charles murmured doubtfully. "I don't pretend to know what you are talking about."

"No, I don't suppose you do," the Earl said, rising. "Be a good fellow now, and run along home to dress. I will pick you up in one hour."

"But I am dressed," Lord Charles protested, glancing down at himself, perplexed.

The Earl smiled. "You cannot possibly expect to accompany me into the country wearing that waistcoat!" he said.

"I won't deny it's a wee bit colorful, but I can't see what that signifies," Lord Charles remarked.

"Ah, but I have my reputation to consider," the Earl replied, leading the way from the room.

Chapter 16

At Twinfriars Adrianna was finding the hours tedious. She had changed into a blue muslin gown following her morning ride and was now seated upon a settee with a book of poems forgotten on her lap. Glancing around Uncle William's gold and scarlet sitting room, she could not help being pleased with the setting, but admitted to herself that she would have liked it better had the Earl been there to share its comfort with her. It seemed so peaceful it was hard to believe that Grimcoe had visited the suite with a fell purpose in view. She had not pursued the subject very far in her mind when it occurred to her that whatever he had been seeking must still be in the room. Just as the Earl had done, she next surmised that Uncle William had somehow come across the papers (if papers there were) and had concealed them in a place of his own contriving.

Thought being the father of action, she jumped to her feet and looked around the room, a little daunted by the sight of so many commodes and cupboards and old coffers. "Where to look?" she asked herself, her eyes coming to rest upon a console table set against the opposite wall. "Well, it's a start," she murmured, crossing to begin an exhaustive search of both the sitting room and bedroom.

An hour later she had ransacked every drawer and shelf in the suite without bringing anything to light. It began to appear that if Uncle William had indeed hidden anything away it must be in some place where it would be unlikely anyone would think to look. If drawers and cupboards were natural hiding places, then what could be considered unnatural choices for concealment? Between the leaves of a book? The thought brought a vision of hundreds of volumes in the library shelves downstairs to her mind, causing her to sit down on the edge of the bed, dismayed. "There is no end to the places where one could look," she had just told herself when her eyes alighted on the Bible reposing upon the bedside table. A moment later she had reached out a hand to pick it up, aware of a feeling of anticipation. "The old fox!" she exclaimed aloud when the leaves fell apart at the pages where the papers had been placed. "The letters were safely under his eye all the while. He knew Grimcoe would evince no interest in the Bible!"

Letters! she thought, surprised. There were five of them, all inscribed to "My darling Lottie" in a hand Adrianna could not remember having seen before. Curious, she turned them over in her fingers, wanting to remove them from their envelopes, but not letting herself succumb. Reading another person's mail was a thing she could not bring herself to do, however great the temptation.

Naturally she needed another hiding place. If she had thought to look in the Bible, Grimcoe might do so himself, another time. She could not repress a start. A secret way into the house had yet to be found. It could not be pleasant, knowing that an intruder was free to come and go at will, with no one the wiser. Shrugging off the thought, she wandered over the suite looking for a place to secrete the letters. It must, of course, be somewhere she had not explored in the course of her own search. She must, she believed, have examined everything in the rooms, with the exception of the art objects on the cabinet shelves. A slow smile came into her eyes. The jades and ivories would be solid, she knew, but the Sevres and Meissen pieces were bound to be hollow, a thing most gentlemen would be unlikely to know, and certainly not a man of Grimcoe's stamp. Not wishing to find it necessary to break the lovely china at some future date in order to extract the letters, she rolled each missive into a slender tube and carefully inserted one of them in each of five Meissen figurines, selecting as her choice those displaying ladies and gentlemen engaged in a musical tableau or swaying in rhythm to the dance. Pleased with her own cunning, she replaced the porcelains upon the shelves and went downstairs to luncheon.

At about this time the Earl, slap up to the mark, was swirling through the village en route to the house, and in general was living up to local expectations in the manner of his return to Twinfriars. While every young fledgling for miles around remained hopeful that a Town Tulip would come among them whom they could ape, and were consequently disappointed when the buttons on his coat did not turn out to be as big as cabbages, still even the most provincial among them knew his lordship to be in the highest kick of fashion the instant of setting eyes on his driving coat with no less than sixteen shoulder-capes. And, to his everlasting credit, the Earl was driving a high-perch phaeton drawn by four prime pieces of the most bang-up bits of blood and bones seen in those parts in many a day.

If the Earl attracted no little attention, the gentleman seated beside him attracted perhaps more. For Lord Charles had elected to clothe his lean frame in a coat with fifteen capes and a double tier of pockets, each of them fastened with one pearl button of extraordinary size. Under this very gratifying evidence of an out-and-outer, displayed by the coat's being flung open, was a waistcoat of green and blue plaid and a cravat of white muslin striped with black. It didn't need the small groom up on his seat behind to know that a pair of top-of-the-trees Corinthians had arrived to enliven the local scene.

"I told you the insignia of the Four-Horse Club would be out of place here," the Earl remarked, turning his team in through the gates of Twinfriars and on to the graveled drive.

"You wear 'em yourself sometimes," Lord Charles grinned, leaning back at ease.

"But only on the main highway, dear boy, only on the main highway," the Earl replied, glancing at his companion's waistcoat and tie. "Damn this drive!"

"Good God!" Lord Charles ejaculated as the phaeton bounced over a particularly deep pothole. "Why, in the name of all that's Holy, don't you get it fixed?"

"I intend to. Now what's the matter?" he added as Lord Charles broke into a shout of laughter.

"By Gad, but that's rich!" Lord Charles gasped.

"Me, wearing the insignia of our club, and on this drive! Blister me if I won't roast you for this for years to come!"

"Do try to exercise a little control," the Earl admonished, pulling up his team before the house. "Adrianna will think I have a madman for friend."

Adrianna would not have believed that the sight of the Earl's handsome face could be so welcome to her. Such had been her irritation of the nerves that she had been unable to suppress a cry upon hearing the crunch of wheels on the gravel out front. Running to a window in time to see the tiger jump down from his perch at the back of the phaeton to run to the horses' heads, she was treated to the sight of two exquisites laughing and clapping each other on the back as they mounted the front steps and passed from her sight. Pervis had opened the door by this time, and a murmur of voices sounded, sending her scurrying back to the settee. By the time the Earl's step was heard approaching the salon door, she had picked up a book and was seemingly absorbed in the printed page.

"You present a pleasingly charming picture, my dear," he said, pausing in the threshold.

"Oh!" Adrianna murmured, feigning a start and then looking up. "I did not hear you come in."

"Did you not, indeed?" he said, strolling forward and amused from not being at all hoodwinked. "I believe you know Lord Charles?"

"Why, yes," she said, laying aside the book and rising to shake hands with their guest. "How do you do?"

"Tolerably," Lord Charles grinned, carrying her fingers to his lips. "I trust we did not disturb you at an exciting time in your reading?"

"No, no," she demurred, flushing slightly. It had just occurred to her that she had been holding the novel upside down. One glance at the Earl sufficed: he had not missed the gaffe.

"You must know I have never been to Twin-friars before," Lord Charles continued. "I had no notion what it would be like."

The Earl's attention had been fixed on Adrianna, but he turned his head at that. "He means the drive, I apprehend," he remarked in some amusement. "He will be happy to discover the house is in better order."

"You are not to listen to him, ma'am," Lord Charles protested. "I never said a thing against the property. Understand you own it now. Ivor's the one who said I'm overdressed—no, that didn't come out right! What I meant—but that don't signify."

"All you meant was that this is the strangest house of your experience," the Earl said, taking snuff. "You are quite right, dear boy. Elegance inside, and a jungle without."

"Pay no attention to him, Lady Ravisham," Lord Charles begged. "He may be somewhat strange at times, but he has never acted this way before, that I know of."

"Ah, but I am in an unusually mellow mood today," the Earl explained, his eyes on Adrianna's face.

She pinked. "Perhaps the origin of the name

'Twinfriars' would interest Lord Charles," she said, leading the conversation into untroubled waters.

"I had wondered about it," Lord Charles grinned. "I would never have thought the limbs on Ivor's family tree would have been sufficiently strong to bear the weight of clergymen among its numbers."

"It was Uncle William's family tree, and you could just be right about that," the Earl replied, an appreciative gleam in his eye.

"Same thing," Lord Charles chuckled in reply.

"It all occurred long before his ancestors came upon the scene," the Earl continued. "The oldest part of the house is reputed to be the remains of a very early monastery founded by a pair of brothers. Our earliest records would appear to bear this out, though whether the friars were actually twins seems unclear. Not that it matters. The story is sufficiently romantic to satisfy the local taste for drama."

Mrs. Chittering appeared in the doorway at that moment, recalling Adrianna to a sense of her responsibilities. "Will you have some refreshment, Lord Charles?" she said. "Sherry? Or perhaps you would prefer something stronger?"

"The sherry will be fine," he smiled.

"Their lordships had better have a whiskey," Mrs. Chittering interposed. "I declare, such a tapping and a pounding as you'd not believe!"

The Earl regarded her without displaying the least surprise. "A search for the hidden entrance has been going forward, I take it," he said.

"Good gracious, sir, I never seen the like!" Mrs. Chittering informed him with a great deal of relish.

"A hidden staircase?" Lord Charles repeated, staring. "Never tell me you are providing me with such an intriguing bit of sport?"

"One does one's poor best," the Earl murmured, smiling.

"Ivor, I could hit you!" Adrianna exclaimed. "Lord Charles will think himself cast adrift in Bedlam!"

"Since you mention it, my dear, Jaimie has a very fair idea of the sort of things that happen here."

"Oh, I say, Lady Ravisham," Lord Charles protested. "Surely you aren't intending to forbid the fun! Speak to her, Ivor, old boy. After that drive down your carriage-way, you owe me!"

The Earl chuckled. "You may search the house from top to bottom, dear boy, if only you will go away."

"Perhaps Ted will like to assist me. Yes, I am sure he will. I cannot think of any reason why he wouldn't."

"Yes," the Earl said. "I am sure Ted is the very one for you. You had better go and enlist his services before he becomes busy in the stables."

"Well, I will, if you won't think it odd, my leaving you so shortly after our arrival."

"I won't think it odd in the least. If I may, I would advise you to start in the attics."

"That's a capital notion. If you are sure—"

"I'm sure. You had best lose no more time in

setting about the search. You will want to make the best use of the daylight while you have it."

"Then I will be off. Don't think I am in any difficulty if I don't appear before dinner."

"I won't," the Earl assured him. "Mrs. Chittering will show you the way upstairs."

Adrianna had turned away some moments before to hide her smiles, and so missed seeing the rapture in Lord Charles's face as he hurried out in Mrs. Chittering's wake. The Earl studied her averted face, then strolled across to her side. "I hope you didn't think me rude," he murmured, putting his hands on her shoulders to turn her about to face him. "I wanted you to myself."

She raised eyes brimful with laughter to his face. "You are become most odious, sir," she gurgled. "Your friend Jaimie has all my sympathy."

"I had no idea the mention of a hidden entrance could produce such amazing results."

"Don't apologize, please. It will keep him amused."

"And out of our hair. Now that we are free from interruption, there is something I want to say to you."

"You used me abominably," she murmured, lowering her eyes.

"I will readily admit I did," he agreed, lifting her face with his fingers under her chin. "Was it so very terrible?"

"That's beside the point," she protested.

"Admit you enjoyed it," he demanded, the devil in his smiling eyes.

She regarded him smolderingly. "You are without a doubt the most maddening, the most—most—"

"Most passionate gentleman of your acquaintance?" he murmured, letting go of her shoulders and sweeping her into his arms.

Lord Charles, reappearing upon the threshold with a question trembling upon his lips, gaped in astonishment at the sight of his hostess locked in his host's embrace. "Oh, I say, old boy," he said. "It ain't proper, kissing in the drawing room. Not in the daytime, it isn't."

The Earl raised his head. "Go away!" he said.

"Well, but—"

"Jaimie, I am a patient man, but I have my limits. Don't press your luck."

"I still say it ain't proper," Lord Charles grinned and took himself off.

"Depraved," Adrianna remarked. "We are both become depraved."

"Yes," the Earl agreed, "I expect we have. Shall we pursue our corruption upstairs?"

"Ivor!"

"And don't tell me I am impossible. I know I am."

"I was going to tell you I have something upstairs to show you."

He first blinked, then gave a shout of laughter. "Have you now?" he said.

"Behave yourself," she shot back. "I meant some letters I found hidden in Uncle William's bedroom."

"Letters!" he repeated, staring.

"In his Bible," she explained.

"Bible?" he said, aghast.

"Really, Ivor, I do wish you would make an attempt to follow my train of thought. I cannot be that vague."

"Pray accept my most humble apologies," he replied, seizing her by the wrist. "You took me by surprise."

"Ivor, what are you about? Where are you taking me? I do wish you would explain instead of pulling me along in this odious way!"

"I am endeavoring to do so, my love," he said, striding across the hall and towing her in his wake. "Allow me to say that you afford me very little opportunity."

"You are a brute," she snapped, drawn irresistibly up the stairs. "Keep this up, and I won't show you the letters!"

"Hid them yourself, did you?" he grinned, opening their sitting room door. "You always were a brat."

"Oh, was I?" she gurgled, waving her arm about. "Guess."

"I don't need to, my dear," he chuckled, taking her in his arms. "I have my own methods. They never fail, I might add."

"Conceited, aren't you?" she said, tilting up her face for his kiss.

"Yes," he murmured, fastening his lips on hers.

"I see what you mean," she chuckled, emerging from the embrace. "I have been very clever, Ivor. I hid them in the porcelains. They are hollow, you know."

"My dear girl, properly brought up young ladies do not gloat," he reprimanded with a twinkle in his eye.

She feigned contrition. "I was not properly brought up," she said. "And besides, I am so very relieved to have them off my hands."

"I beg you will signify your relief in a more becoming manner," he said, having the last word. "May I ask: the Sevres, or the Meissen?"

"The Meissen. Could you be jealous of my success?"

The Earl crossed to the display cabinet. "My remarks appear to have produced a strange effect upon your intellect," he said, picking up a figurine and peering into the hole in its bottom. "How do you plan to remove the letters?"

"Let me fish them out," she replied, taking the ceramic into her own keeping. "Whose letters are they?"

"My dear, you cannot expect me to tell you that," he said, watching her extract the missives from their hiding place.

"I don't see that you are being fair," she remarked, pausing in her task.

"Little in life is fair, my love," he replied, advancing upon her around a chair.

She thrust the letters behind her back. "I found them all by myself, and now you will not tell me why they are so important," she said, retreating a step.

He continued to stalk her. "It is not my place to do so," he replied in a tone that she could not think sounded very regretful.

"That does not altogether surprise me," she gurgled, ducking under his outstretched arms and darting across the room. "They aren't yours, are they?"

"No, dearest," he replied, refusing to go chasing after her. "My darling's name isn't Lottie."

"What will you do with them?" she asked after a moment.

"Restore them to their owner."

"I would like to be present when you return them to Lord Charles," she said with a perfectly straight face.

"You are fishing," he chuckled, opening wide his arms.

Adrianna cast herself into them and flung her arms around his neck. "I seem to have caught a large one," she murmured and raised her lips to his.

"Ah, but only because I like the bait," he said, sweeping her off her feet and carrying her to the bed.

Chapter 17

Lord Belderbrock, as it happened, had no idea
that anyone could be on his trail. Not dreaming
that the Earl had gained knowledge of the blackmailing scheme, he had seen no need to make
haste in conducting Grimcoe on a further search
of Twinfriars. There being no one to tell him that
the Countess of Ravisham was in residence there,
he had put off the chore for several days, partly
from indolence, and partly from a perfectly understandable aversion to Grimcoe's company. Thus
it was in no particularly pleasurable frame of mind
that he set out with his henchman upon the ride
to Twinfriars from his temporary lodgings at a
local inn. By one of those strange quirks of fate
which seem to dog the footsteps of fools and the
weakhearted, the date selected chanced to coin-
cide, not only with the Earl's arrival, but with
Adrianna's mild attack of insomnia as well. Per-

haps a dog barking in the distance had awakened her. Or perhaps it had been that very quality of hushed stillness which was bound to attract notice that had disturbed her rest. Whatever the cause, Lord Belderbrock could not have been expected to reckon with the wife of the Earl's bosom being at a kitchen window in the dead of night, staring out at heaven only knew what. Not only had she become so lost to all sense of propriety as to creep downstairs in search of food when she should have been upstairs in bed, cuddled against the Earl and fast asleep, she was utterly destroying Grimcoe's chances of success by partaking of her snack by moonlight. Not so much as a pinpoint of light flickered a warning to any watching eyes.

Grimcoe had some years before arrived at that stage in life when, having given up all hope that great wealth would somehow miraculously drop plump into his lap, he had come to accept the more limited expectations that seem the destiny of most men. For this reason, it was with only tepid interest that he stole from shadow to shadow, gliding ever closer to the waiting house. From his vast store of experience gleaned in the course of a checkered career, he knew that Lord Belderbrock, waiting in his coach a safe distance from the scene, would grab the lion's share of their portion of the blackmail money for himself. Had his lordship but known it, a henchman with no real stake in an enterprise must be viewed in the light of being a poor risk. And so it proved. Grimcoe, from having no real conviction that a heavy purse would in very truth come his way, grew careless. Adrianna, idly looking out upon the landscape, caught a telltale glimpse of his shadowy form darting behind a tree.

With a gasp of surprise, she shrank back behind the curtains, her heart beating fast, and breathlessly strained her eyes. Moments passed before a faint suggestion of movement in the shadows informed her she had indeed seen a stealthy visitor. Taking care to remain out of sight, she watched the unknown's halting approach until he at last melted into the area of dense darkness cast upon the scene by the bulk of the house. Although her mouth felt a little dry, she was more intrigued than frightened. A tiny scrabbling sound, followed by the faint squeak of a door being swung open on protesting hinges, came faintly to her ears. There could be no doubt about it: The tangle of shrubbery hugging the foundation walls most assuredly concealed a long unused, and so forgotten, access to the cellars. Apparently satisfied that Twinfriars' occupants slept, Grimcoe had unknowingly revealed the secret of his past nocturnal ransacking of the house.

Adrianna took care to move quietly herself. Carrying her slippers in her hands, she stole across the kitchen floor to the door into the hall. Resolutely keeping a tight rein on her nerves, she slowly opened it a crack and slipped through, with only a whisper of sound to mark her passing. Pausing, she waited an agonizing moment, listening intently, before creeping on down the hall, her bare feet making no sound on the wood floor. Arriving at the foot of the stairs, she tested each step for any treacherous creaking of the boards and went slowly upward from tread to tread, hugging the wall and letting the handrail take some of her weight to lessen the possibility of any betraying noise. The climb of the stairs accomplished, she exhaled a silent sigh of relief and sped on down the hall to awaken the Earl.

Roused from sleep still groggy by a highly excited rendition of events poured into his ears, he could at first but little credit the tale. "The fool's returned, you say," he muttered, sitting up.

"Ivor, of course he has!" she hissed, her eyes aglow with a thirst for adventure. "He is in the cellars at this very moment! I am positive he is, so don't you go putting me off. What are you going to do?"

"Collar the fellow," he replied, casting off the covers and reaching for his robe. "I'm damned if I will have him creeping about under my very nose."

"That's an excellent notion," she approved, sitting down upon her elegant little French chair to put her slippers back on. "But we had better hurry!"

"You are not leaving this room, my girl. Get that through your head," he said, thrusting his feet into his houseshoes. "Lord, but I wish I had a gun!"

"There are pistols in that cupboard," she said, jumping up and running across the room to rummage on the shelves. "I came across them while searching for the letters," she explained, brandishing a gun in each hand.

"Be careful!" he almost shouted in his alarm. "They may be loaded!"

"Yes, I rather think they are," she said, turning a firearm about in her fingers and examining it with care. "I can see a little rounded end peeking out just there."

"Don't point that barrel at your face!" he cried, striding forward to snatch the pistols from her hands. "For God's sake, Adrianna! They are primed and cocked!"

"I know how to shoot it," she protested. "I didn't have my finger on that little thingamajig one pulls."

"You are enough to try the patience of a saint," he said, exasperated. "Get back in that bed, and stay there!"

"No!" she objected. "I am coming with you."

"You step one foot through that door and it will be much the worse for you!" he warned her grimly. "Which room did you put Jaimie in?"

"The yellow bedchamber. Ivor—"

"Under no circumstances!" he replied, striding across the room. "Close and lock this door behind me, and do not open it for anyone!"

"Not even for you?" she said, and found herself talking to empty space.

She very sensibly waited until she was reasonably certain that the Earl and Lord Charles had gone downstairs; then she went to the cupboard for a third gun. It was heavier and therefore more unwieldy than the dueling pistols carried by the men, but she felt sure that it too was loaded. Holding the firearm out before her, with her finger crooked around the trigger, she stole out into the hall and paused, waiting for her eyes to grow accustomed to the dark. Satisfied that she was following along behind the Earl, she crept along the passageway to the staircase and started down it, aware that she was enjoying herself immensely.

The Earl and Lord Charles, meanwhile, had reached the landing at the top of the cellar stairs. Peering downward into the black void below, they paused to listen intently for any sound disturbing the absolute quiet of the darkness. Hearing nothing, the Earl moved forward a cautious step, with Lord Charles right beside him. Lord Charles's foot collided suddenly with a pail and mop left upon the landing by Mrs. Chittering, sending it clattering down the steps and creating a terrible din as it bounced from side to side.

The results were immediate and startling. The Earl swore mightily, while behind him a shadowy figure shot through the library door and ran across the main hall. The sound of bolts on the front door being desperately drawn back had scarcely had time to die away when Adrianna, transfixed halfway down the main staircase, uttered a piercing scream and wildly fired her gun in the general direction of the figure silhouetted in the moonlit open door. Before the loud report had time in its turn to die away, the intruder sank slowly to his knees and pitched forward onto his face.

The Earl erupted through the kitchen door and

tore down the hall, fear clutching at his heart. "Adrianna, where are you?" he shouted at the top of his lungs while running toward the stairs.

"I'm here," she called, rushing down the remaining steps and flinging herself into his arms.

"Who fired that shot?" he demanded, weak with relief to find her safe. "I told you to lock yourself in your room. You could have been killed!"

"Well, I wasn't," she said in a tone the Earl could only think pert.

"You had better relieve her of that gun," Lord Charles advised from the background. "It is pointed directly at your head, old chap."

The Earl's brows shot up. "How is this?" he said, taking the pistol from her limp grasp. "May I inquire what the devil you are doing with a gun in your hand?"

"Shooting Grimcoe," she admitted, turning in his arms to point to the still form huddled in the open threshold.

"Good God!" the Earl ejaculated, staring at Grimcoe's body stretched out on the floor.

"Someone had to shoot him," she defended herself. "You certainly were making a botch of things, between the two of you."

"Someone left a mop-pail on the landing," Lord Charles explained ruefully. "I fell over it."

"I should think you could watch where you are going," Adrianna commented. "I," she added, stressing the pronoun, "watched where I was going."

"But then," said the Earl, "you have the advantage of feminine intuition on your side. We poor males must just bumble around as best we might, even if that bumbling means our death."

"I shouldn't think that Grimcoe is dead," Adrianna protested.

"I shouldn't be surprised if he is very dead," the Earl commented rather dryly.

"I have never fired a gun before in my life," Adrianna confessed somewhat needlessly. "I must have hit him by the merest chance."

The Earl eyed Grimcoe's huddled form. "At this range, you could hardly miss," he said.

"But I didn't aim the gun, Ivor, not really," Adrianna protested. "I just pulled that little thing that—well—that one does pull. I don't even know the name of it."

"It would appear you do not need to know," the Earl remarked dryly.

"Don't you think you should see if he is seriously wounded?"

"If he were, he would not be groaning."

By this time the Chitterings and Pervis had come hurrying down the stairs to discover the cause of the commotion. Mrs. Chittering, saying she had experience with gunshot wounds, and begging her ladyship's pardon, took charge. Grimcoe was carried to a sofa and his wound laid bare. Mrs. Chittering announced it trifling, much to Adrianna's relief, and staunched the flow of blood. Binding a pad tightly in place, she said, "Likely that will do for the time being. The ball will need to come out, but it can wait till morning, if need be."

The Earl, meanwhile, had beckoned the footman

to his side. "You will go for the doctor, Pervis, at once."

"Yes, my lord."

"Further, you will inform the Constable that he is needed here. I have no intention of granting sanctuary to a criminal. He belongs in gaol."

Chittering, nettled to find Pervis taking preference over himself, took a surly tone. "There's no sayin' as how this night's work come about," he growled. "That there front door was locked, you can lay yer life on it, me lord. I bolted it meself."

The Earl considered a reprimand, then shrugged. It was an unsettling night for them all. "It seems there is a door from the outside into the cellars," he explained. "We will seal it off tomorrow."

"I must say I will sleep better from knowing the house is secured," Adrianna remarked, hugging her robe more closely about herself to ward off the chill.

The Earl noted the gesture and crossed to her side. "The intrusion was unexpected, but there is nothing now to disturb your rest," he said. "Go back to bed, my dear. There is nothing left for you to do down here."

"But the Constable may wish to question me," she protested, though reeling with fatigue.

"He can do so tomorrow just as easily as tonight," the Earl replied. "Mrs. Chittering will be up shortly with a glass of warm milk. Run along now, there's a good girl."

And so Adrianna, exhausted with the excitement and emotional upheavals of the past hour, was tucked up between the sheets, given the warm milk, and left alone to sleep.

When she awoke, the morning was far advanced and the house quiet. The Earl had evidently been listening for the first sounds that she was awake, for the door between their bedrooms promptly opened, and he came in. "Feeling better?" he said, crossing to sit down upon the edge of her bed.

"I feel rested, if that is what you mean," she replied, propping herself up with a pillow at her back. "What has happened, Ivor? Did the Constable ask for me?"

"He won't need to question you, my dear. I gave him a full accounting. It seems Grimcoe is well known to our local magistrate."

"Then he is alive?"

"You only winged him, Adrianna. The doctor came while you slept, and took the bullet out. He is now reposing in the local gaol, awaiting his trial. Constable Mumfry assures me it will not be necessary for you to appear. You can give your testimony by a deposition."

"That is kind of them. I hope never to see Grimcoe again."

"I hope you won't harbor any feeling of guilt over this."

"No, why should I? If I hadn't shot him, he would have escaped. I'm not saying I relished it, but I cannot regret it either."

"I am glad you feel that way. Grimcoe was a very pretty rogue who deserved his fate."

"There is more to it than that, Ivor. Who owned the letters, and why was Grimcoe searching for them? Do you know?"

"I do, my dear."

"Well, it is only fair that you should tell me. I have been involved in the affair almost from the beginning, I think, and I still don't know what it is about. At the least, you might clear up my confusion over the lady named Lottie."

"No, my dear. I can tell you that Lottie hardly personifies anyone's concept of a lady, but beyond that, I am not at liberty."

"But I would be discreet."

He smiled and rose. "I think you are trying to force my hand," he said. "What would you say if I permit you to gallop before breakfast?"

She dimpled. "I do believe you are attempting to drive a bargain with me, sir," she said. "Very well. I surrender. I have been longing to since the day you first put me aboard a horse."

So they galloped together on the smooth turf of the lawns before the house until he felt confident she was capable of negotiating more uneven ground. For the next two days they explored the countryside, usually accompanied by Lord Charles, and among those who were privileged to glimpse the handsome trio, a good deal of excitement was felt. It soon became evident that the ladies of the district, along with the younger of the gentlemen, were torn between hopes of a round of social entertainments occurring at Twinfriars, and fear of not receiving an invitation themselves.

Due to the efforts of Adrianna, Twinfriars, so long bereft of gaiety and charm, began to take on a more cheerful air. The draperies were pulled back to let in the sunlight, and great bowls of flowers scented the air. Chairs were rearranged to provide intimate areas for conversation, and plump cushions appeared on the sofas, inviting repose. Amid such pleasant surroundings, the night of Grimcoe's return quickly faded from Adrianna's mind.

Chapter 18

For several days after that same evening, Lord Belderbrock kept to his room at the Jackstraws Inn, a shaken and apprehensive intriguer. Having conceived a fear that the Earl had somehow divined his connection with Grimcoe, he hesitated to venture forth and spent much of his time peering from his window or straining his ears for the first sound of carriage wheels out front. As might have been expected, such very odd conduct could not fail to attract the notice of the innkeeper. Coggin and his wife had one thing in common; they shared a love of gossip. They not only discussed the matter between themselves, they shared their speculations with all and sundry who happened into their establishment. By dint of dwelling tediously and often on his lordship's peculiarities, they soon made him the talk of the countryside. Had Belderbrock but known it, his newly hired groom, who had been recommended by Lord Chester, was actually a servant of Lord Chester and had been placed in his employ to spy on him. Thus it was soon brought to Lord Chester's ears that his coconspirator spent much of his time cowering in his room, a situation frought with peril in Lord Chester's mind.

When several days had passed without the Earl putting in an appearance at the inn, Lord Belderbrock became convinced that he had scant cause for fear. Grimcoe, although reposing in gaol with his wound on the mend, had maintained a judicious silence. These agreeable reflections brought him a certain comfort, but were soon put to flight by the unwanted arrival of Lord Chester at the inn.

Lord Belderbrock had not the smallest intention of acknowledging his lordship's visit, and sent word downstairs by his valet that he was indisposed. His relief at having seen Lord Chester step down from the coach drawn up out front had been immediately banished by the thought that he might just fare better at the hands of the Earl. Ravisham might be a force to reckon with, but there was a certain evil about Chester which Ravisham lacked. Confident at having forestalled a confrontation he had no desire to sustain, he took up his by now customary position at the window and waited to see Lord Chester reenter his coach preparatory to departing.

His tormentor's voice brought his head around. "I am sorry to find you indisposed," Lord Chester remarked in silken tones as he walked into the room and closed the door.

Belderbrock fairly goggled. "I told my man I could not see you," he gasped, alarmed.

"So he said. You will admit it was an odd thing to do," Lord Chester replied, his smile not quite reaching his eyes. "Surely you would expect me to hurry to your side."

"No, why should I?" Belderbrock parried, eyeing him in some trepidation.

"But I understand you have been keeping to your room," Lord Chester purred, laying his hat and cane down upon a chest. "I will admit to a certain curiosity, my dear Belderbrock. You must be desperate indeed."

"Oh, as to that, there isn't much to do in this place. It is quite provincial, you know."

"You relieve me greatly," Lord Chester murmured, pulling a chair forward and sitting down. "Do tell me all about the things you have not been doing in this place."

"I am sure I don't know why you are so interested," Lord Belderbrock temporized, wondering how long it would take Chester to get around to Grimcoe.

He was not to be left long in doubt. His lordship's brows rose. "If I were not, I should not be here now," he said. "As you may know, it is not my custom to make calls."

"Well, I didn't ask you to come," Lord Belderbrock found the courage to snap.

"From your attitude, I would surmise something has gone amiss," Lord Chester remarked, his eyes, cold as steel, staring across at him.

Belderbrock plunged a hand into a pocket and removed his snuff box, his fingers shaking slightly. "Amiss?" he quavered. "Why should you think that?"

Lord Chester leaned forward in his chair. "Enough of this!" he flung at him. "What happened at Twinfriars?"

Belderbrock seemed to shrink. "At Twinfriars?" he repeated, desperately searching his mind.

"You took Grimcoe there," Lord Chester prompted. "What happened?"

Lord Belderbrock shuddered. "I—I really don't know," he admitted, taking a pinch of snuff and spilling much of it down his waistcoat.

"You don't know!" Lord Chester demanded explosively.

Lord Belderbrock reddened. "I took him to a spot fairly closer to the house where my coach would be out of sight, and set him down. No one was about and the house was dark. There was a moon, but that didn't signify. Grimcoe kept to the shadows. Good God! How was I to know he would be shot!"

"Shot!" Lord Chester uttered sharply.

"He was taking a long time about it, but I waited," Lord Belderbrock chattered. "I was near to leaving, but I stayed!"

"What a disconcerting time it must have been for you," Lord Chester remarked sarcastically.

Lord Belderbrock drew himself up short. "That is easy for you to say. You weren't sitting out there alone, expecting to be accosted at any moment. I suppose you would have hung around yourself after you heard a pistol fired!"

"No, there you are wrong," Lord Chester replied with a touch of feigned affability. "I would have removed myself from the vicinity without delay. Pray, what did you do next?"

"I came straight here."

"Where you have remained in seclusion ever since. I imagine it has not occurred to you to discover Grimcoe's fate."

"Now, there you are wrong," Lord Belderbrock shot back with a great deal of satisfaction. "The entire inn is abuzz with it. He is lodged in the local gaol, his wound on the mend. I heard it was Lady Ravisham who shot him, but that is all I've heard."

"And you think the local tattles will have gotten wind of it if Grimcoe has elected to save his miserable skin by sacrificing yours?"

This reference to his own vulnerability in the affair caused Belderbrock to blanch. "The Constable comes here at least twice a day for his pint. He would have said so, if Grimcoe had talked."

"You seem strangely sure of that," Lord Chester remarked.

"Well, what would you have me do? Tear my hair?"

"At the moment I have no intention of disclosing what I would have you do. You seem to have a propensity for making a hash of things, but I shan't permit that to upset my plans."

"What are you going to do? If Ravisham is on to us—"

"On to you, my dear Belderbrock. On to you. There are always more plans to be made, and I intend to have those letters. Perhaps Ravisham will prove useful after all."

"Do walk right up to him and ask for them," Belderbrock said cordially. "I wish you will make him aware of what Twinfriars hides. He will like to know, I'm sure. But you would not get the letters then, now would you? Ravisham would keep the windfall for himself."

"Little you understand his lordship, my good fool. He would turn the letters over to Lord Charles and never bat an eye. Honor has ever been a virtue with the Earl, I promise you."

Lord Belderbrock stared. "You have become obsessed by those letters!" he said.

"No," Lord Chester replied indifferently. "My creditors have become obsessed with me."

"I'll take your word for that. Do make Ravisham a scene, and then come back and tell me all about it. I will be waiting."

"You will, but, alas, not here. You are coming away with me. I shan't be caught napping with you a third time."

And so it chanced that they had cleared the

outskirts of the village and were on their way down the main highway at a smart pace when Adrianna came along on the verge beside the road toward them. She was riding sidesaddle, an art the Earl had insisted she master, and was trailed at a discreet distance by a groom. She saw them at once and pulled her horse to a halt, undecided until the expression on Lord Chester's face claimed her notice. Something in the malevolence of his stare sent a stab of fear through her. Wheeling her mount, she dug her heel into the mare's flank, sending the horse surging across a field toward the concealing trees of a wood, her startled groom setting out in hot pursuit.

Back in the coach, Lord Belderbrock gazed after her retreating back, perplexed. "What d'you think came over her?" he said.

"She recognized me," Lord Chester replied.

Lord Belderbrock transferred his gaze to Lord Chester's face. "Does that matter?" he asked.

"Apparently our fair Countess knows more of our affairs than I would have dreamt. I have been caught napping, it seems. I should never have been seen abroad with you."

Lord Belderbrock gave a sudden chortle. "They will be on to you now too," he said. "How does it feel to squirm?"

The arrow hit home, as Belderbrock hoped it would. "It appears I have more of a task before me than I thought," Lord Chester remarked in a somewhat strange tone.

Lord Belderbrock stared at him. "What do you

mean by that?" he demanded, frightened somehow, but striving not to show it.

"I make you my compliments, but you will never know," Lord Chester replied. "It brings an apt quote to mind. 'Lie down with dogs, get up with fleas,' I believe the saying goes."

"You are talking nonsense," Lord Belderbrock accused. "We were both caught napping, but I don't blather trite phrases over it."

"Accept my apologies," Lord Chester replied, a gleam of amusement in his eyes. "Perhaps you will find tonight's activities more to your liking. I have arranged a little entertainment for you, which I trust you will approve."

"I should think we have too much on our minds to think of amusements. Grimcoe—"

"Ah, yes, Grimcoe," Lord Chester interrupted. "The very pith and heart of our concern. He will be lonely and in need of cheering up. We will ease his solitude, never forgetting to provide the—er, cheer."

"You mean to visit him?" Belderbrock asked, appalled.

"But in secret, sir, in secret. His place of incarceration will no doubt possess a window opening to the rear. Country gaols always do. By lowering a bottle of wine to him on a string, we will insure his devotion to us until his dying day," Lord Chester concluded, chuckling.

Lord Belderbrock prided himself (falsely) upon being adept at sizing up his man, but he could not rid himself of the idea that when up against a fellow of Chester's stamp, he stood very little chance.

It would be best not to cross him, he decided; having gone along this far, he could hardly object now to going the rest of the way.

So it was that darkness found him pressed against the rear wall of a smelly gaol. Gad, what a stench, he thought, cautiously raising his head to peer in over the sill of the high window. It was barred, but open to the breeze, he was glad to see. "Hsst!" he breathed to attract Grimcoe's notice. "I have a bottle of wine for you," he whispered, pushing it in between the bars and lowering it on a string. "See you don't drop it, now!"

"Don't worry, I won't," Grimcoe whispered in his turn, snatching the bottle with eager hands.

Lord Belderbrock listened to the gurgle of the liquid as Grimcoe tilted the wine down his throat. "You haven't talked, have you?" he said, obvious worry in his voice. "We can't have that, you know."

"No," Grimcoe replied, taking another deep draught. "Just bring me a bottle tomorrow night, me hearty, and mum's the word, I promise you."

"I will be back after dark," Lord Belderbrock assured him, melting away into the shadows.

"Did he drink it?" Lord Chester demanded the instant Belderbrock reentered the coach.

"He has emptied the bottle by now, and who can blame him? He will shortly be willing to say or do anything to escape from that hole."

Lord Chester gave his coachman the office to proceed and lounged back in his corner, a thin smile curving his mouth. Belderbrock could have no notion of the thoughts revolving in his brain.

Had he had so much as an inkling, he would have leapt from the rapidly moving vehicle with no thought of injury. As it was, he calmly leaned back in his own corner and rode to his death with a smirk upon his lips.

The coach turned off the highway onto a country lane and drew to a halt. The groom climbed down from the box, the steps were let down, and the door wrenched open. "Here, what's this!" Lord Belderbrock ejaculated, sitting up to peer out into the moonlight.

"A celebration of sorts," Lord Chester replied, stepping down with a bottle of wine in his hand.

"Out here?" Lord Belderbrock said, aghast.

"Why not?" Lord Chester replied, strolling away to sit down upon a log. "The coach is stuffy."

"I never heard of anything to equal this!" Lord Belderbrock asserted, stubbornly refusing to budge.

"Please do not enact a scene before my servants," Lord Chester sneered. "Come and join me in a drink before you make a complete ass of yourself."

Belderbrock glanced at the expressionless lackey waiting to assist him to the ground, and flushed. "Oh, very well," he said, stalking across to the log. "Surely you aren't expecting me to drink from the bottle?"

"But, of course, my dear fellow," Lord Chester said in the friendliest tone imaginable. "I haven't a glass, I'm afraid. No, no, after you, Belderbrock. You are my guest."

Lord Belderbrock fastidiously wiped the neck

of the bottle with a clean handkerchief. "Cheers," he said and drank.

"A good vintage, would you not say?" Lord Chester smiled, then pushed back the bottle when Belderbrock would have passed it across to him. "Have another nip, old boy. I insist."

Lord Belderbrock tipped back his head and swallowed a few further mouthfuls. "If this were my last drink, I would not ask for better," he said expansively.

Lord Chester rose. "That is fortunate, since it is," he remarked, walking away.

"Is what?" Lord Belderbrock asked, completely at sea.

"Your last drink, you bungling fool. Did you think I would leave you at large to put a noose around my neck? The wine is laced with cyanide."

"Eh? What's that?" Lord Belderbrock cried, stunned.

"It is a poison, I'm told. Say your prayers, dear boy. One must prepare oneself to meet one's maker, you know. I judge you have less than five minutes in which to do so."

"Grimcoe?" Lord Belderbrock gasped, horror starting from his eyes.

His lordship bowed. "As you say, Grimcoe. Such a pity, murder and suicide. But then, you know that, I daresay, since you have just committed both," he added, stepping into his coach without a backward glance.

The groom closed the door, let up the steps, and climbed up onto the box again. Having settled himself, he turned his head and goggled fascinated at the figure writhing in horrible pain on the grass behind them. "Gawd," he breathed. "Did ye ever see the like!"

"Don't look," the coachman growled, grimly setting his horses forward. "It ain't a pretty sight."

"Is he dying?" the groom quavered, the reality of the gruesome scene brought home to him at last.

"Keep your tongue in your head, my boy," the coachman advised. "You'll live longer if you do."

"But, 'tis murder!" the groom gasped, licking his lips.

"Don't let his lordship hear ye talk like that. He don't take kindly to gabby servants."

The groom drew a deep breath and covered his ears in a vain attempt to muffle the dreadful screams receding in the distance. "Gawd!" he breathed again, shuddering.

Chapter 19

Early the following afternoon Adrianna rode out with Lord Charles's tiger, Ted, for groom. Since the Earl was away attending a prize fight with his lordship, she had rummaged in a cupboard for her breeches and shirt in rebellion against riding sidesaddle. The London servants would of a certainty have been shocked to see her descending the stairs dressed in boy's clothing, but luckily Pervis was the only footman on duty in the hall. He had quickly become a great admirer of Simpson, and had just as quickly sought to imitate the schooled impassivity of the butler's bearing. The results were mixed. At times he remembered to keep his eyes carefully averted in cool detachment to the world around him, at other times his eyes twinkled merrily. On this occasion it proved to be the former. Contriving to gaze magnificently at a spot somewhere just beyond Adrianna's shoulder, he bowed and opened the door for her, and thereby missed the smile she was unable to hide.

The encounter put her in a playful mood. A very playful mood, unfortunately. No sooner was she halfway across the field that separated Twinfriars' grounds from the woodland than she looked back over her shoulder at Ted trailing along a discreet distance behind, and chuckled in an excess of joy at the feeling of freedom her breeches gave her. The groom gaped in surprise when she sent her horse into a gallop, then sent his mount thundering after her. Adrianna straightaway leaned forward over the mare's neck and tore onward toward the wood, entering the trees at full tilt. Ted was quickly left behind with no clear notion of which trail to follow. "Your ladyship!" he cried, pushing through the undergrowth.

Adrianna's laughter echoed through the gloom, affording him an opportunity to follow her progress through the wood. She led him a merry chase, dodging in and out among the trees until the growth began to thin and she found herself coming out onto the highway. "Here, Ted," she called, dropping into a canter.

She had not gone far along the road when she heard a coach coming up fast behind her. Moving over to the verge, she drew her horse to a halt and turned her head to idly watch the vehicle pass on by. To her utter astonishment, the conveyance came to a lurching stop beside her and the groom jumped down. By now thoroughly alarmed, she backed her mount, but he was too quick for her. She was dragged from her horse, the door of the coach was wrenched open, and she found herself staring into Lord Chester's hateful countenance. "You!" she gasped, struggling to free herself from the groom's grasp.

"What a fortunate circumstance," Lord Chester remarked, motioning to his lackey. "I have been contemplating how best to bring about a meeting with you."

"Kindly instruct your servant to unhand me," she shot back, only to find herself hauled forward by the groom.

"But I have a great desire to pursue your acquaintance," Lord Chester purred.

"Well, I have no desire to pursue yours," she snapped.

"I am desolated," he smiled. "Jack, if you please."

Before she could think, she was propelled into the coach and flung to the seat. She was up in a flash, desperately fighting to escape and screaming Ted's name at the top of her lungs. To no avail. Lord Chester delivered a stunning blow to the side of her head, sending her crashing to the seat, only vaguely aware that the coach had lurched forward at great speed.

Ted, meanwhile, had burst from the wood just in time to catch a glimpse of the coach disappearing in the direction of the village some two and a half miles away. The sound of her ladyship's screams, coupled with the sight of her horse cropping the grass beside the road, and he knew the worst. He had no idea who had seized her ladyship, or why, but he had no doubt she was in that coach. Digging his heels into his horse's flanks, he set out in pursuit, galloping wildly down the road. When he came at last to the outskirts of the village, however, there was no sight of the faster team.

An elderly resident was sitting on a bench before his cottage, dozing in the sun. "You, there," the groom called. "Have ye seen a coach passing this way?"

The old gentleman pointed with a bony finger. "A big one, it was," he muttered, fixing the groom with a rheumy eye. "Went smack through old Brownie's cabbage patch, he did."

"How long ago?" Ted demanded.

"A right smart time now, laddie. Ye'll never catch up to him."

Ted, resigning himself to the inevitable, turned his horse about and set off at a walk to collect her ladyship's mare on his return to Twinfriars.

By four o'clock the entire household was worried. The Earl and Lord Charles had not returned, and Simpson did not quite know what to make of Ted's story. Under ordinary circumstances her ladyship might be expected to be taken up by friends, but it was unlike her not to alert the groom; this fact, coupled with Ted's report of having heard her scream, lent credence to his tale. Urged to do so by Mrs. Chittering, at length Simpson sent a lackey in search of the Earl. Around five o'clock the groom returned, riding beside his lordship and Lord Charles. The Earl went swiftly up the steps and into the hall and found himself face to face with the majority of the staff. Mrs. Chittering was collapsed upon a chair, a footman vigorously fanning the air a few scant inches from her face. Simpson looked harassed, and several young housemaids were sobbing in the background.

"Mrs. Chittering, Simpson, and Ted, this way, if you please. The rest of you, go about your business," the Earl said, leading the way to his study.

The young groom broke into a spate of words. "Her ladyship screamed, my lord, I'm sure she did!" he concluded, having come to the end of his tale. "I could never be mistaken about a thing like that!"

The Earl laid his whip and glove on a table. "And where were you while all of this was taking place?" he asked.

Ted hung his head. "Her ladyship—we were—I guess ye could say we were playing hide-and-seek, my lord."

The Earl's jaw dropped. "Hide-and-seek?" he said. "Nonsense!"

Mrs. Chittering wrung her hands. "Nasty boy!" she cried, the tears rolling down her cheeks. "You were put to watching over her ladyship, not to play games!"

"Pray, Mrs. Chittering, dry your tears," the Earl begged. "I am sure there is some simple explanation to account for what has occurred."

"It's not like her ladyship to play off tricks on us," Mrs. Chittering averred, the tears breaking out afresh. "Her ladyship wouldn't be one to worry us like this. No, mark my words, sir, some evil has befallen my lady."

Lord Charles turned a sapient eye upon the housekeeper. "Madam, do strive for control," he said. "You will not help her ladyship by carrying on like this."

"That's a fact, my lord," Mrs. Chittering sniffed. "What with the excitement and all, I don't know whether I'm before or behind."

"Then I suggest you find yourself," Lord Charles replied sardonically.

Whereupon the Earl intervened. "Be quiet, both of you," he said. "Ted, have you any idea where the coach was headed?"

"The old gentleman pointed down the road toward London, my lord, but it could be anywhere. Roads turn off the main highway every few miles, as I'm sure your lordship knows."

"Yes, I do know. We will inquire at every turning. Someone will have been curious enough to note a coach's passing."

A tap came upon the study door. "Excuse me, my lord, but the Constable has arrived," a footman announced.

"I knew it!" Mrs. Chittering cried with sufficient force to startle them all.

"Show him in," the Earl said. "Mrs. Chittering, I must ask you to cease your lamentations."

"But what can a policeman be wanting here, my lord?"

"Suppose we let him tell us," the Earl replied, turning toward the door as the Constable came hurrying in. "Ah, good afternoon, Constable Mumfry."

"Good afternoon, my lord. I must ask you to forgive this intrusion."

"Not at all. What can I do for you?"

"Grimcoe is dead, my lord."

The Earl became very still. "Indeed?" he said. "How?"

"Poisoned wine, my lord. Someone passed a bottle to him through a window in his cell."

"You are going to say, I think, that you have no witnesses."

"None, my lord."

"Ah, but one may be mistaken. I believe there is a saying that the higher they climb, the farther they fall."

"My lord?"

"I suggest you question a rogue by the name of Lord Belderbrock. I am afraid I am unable to furnish you with his present whereabouts."

"Lord Belderbrock?" the Constable repeated, startled. "His lordship's body was found this morning, my lord."

"So?" the Earl murmured, his eyes hard as agates. "You interest me profoundly. Belderbrock was himself a victim of poisoned wine, I apprehend?"

"Of a certainty, my lord. It seems logical to assume there is a connection between the two deaths."

"You want to know if by any chance I might have some idea of what it could be."

Lord Charles broke in. "One thing we do know, Ivor. The coach could not have been Belderbrock's."

239

"I could almost wish it were," the Earl replied dryly. "At least we would have had a starting point."

"Adrianna is very likely with friends," Lord Charles continued buoyantly. "The more I think of it, the more certain I become."

"Your efforts are most praiseworthy, Jaimie, but Adrianna is virtually unacquainted in these parts."

"I would have thought that myself, but we may be mistaken. Ask Ted, here. He usually knows what's afoot."

The tiger looked thoughtful, then shook his head. "I never seen her ladyship do more than nod to anyone, my lord. She was always friendly-like, but there weren't no cause for more."

At this moment the footman rapped again and entered. "A Mr. Brown from the village, my lord, desires speech with your lordship."

The Earl turned his head. "I am not at liberty," he said. "He may return another day."

"Excuse me, my lord," the tiger interrupted, "but the old villager spoke of someone called Brownie who saw the coach."

"Show him in," the Earl instructed the lackey, then stepped forward when a stooped old gentleman was ushered through the door.

"Ye the Earl?" the man asked, fixing his lordship with angry eyes.

"I am," the Earl acknowledged.

"What was yer coachman about, adrivin' through me cabbage patch?" the villager demanded, not mincing words. "Swung round the corner right through it, 'e did!"

The Earl opened his eyes at him. "Your cabbage patch?" he said. "I am much afraid I have no idea what you are talking about."

"Me cabbage patch!" Mr. Brown repeated in a voice that brooked no nonsense. "Yer coach run right through it, sir!"

"I am desolated, Mr.—er, Brown, but I must inform you that, if some coach—er, ran through your cabbages, it certainly was not my coach."

"Ye said ye be the Earl!"

"I did," the Earl confessed.

"Then 'twas yer coach!" Mr. Brown said positively.

Lord Charles burst out laughing. "Lord, Ivor," he gasped, "I'm dashed if I'll let you hear the last of this! Cabbages!" he added, going off into another peal of merriment.

"That will do, Jaimie," the Earl murmured, hard put to conceal his own amusement.

"It come from this direction," Mr. Brown insisted, not giving an inch.

A sudden quiet came upon the room. "Come now," the Constable said, breaking it. "You cannot accuse his lordship's coachman—"

"I can, and do!" snapped Mr. Brown. "Me cabbages be ruint!"

"Forget your damned vegetables for the moment," the Earl said. "I am more interested in the coach. Describe it, if you will be so good."

"Forget me cabbages!" Mr. Brown repeated, stunned. "More interested in the coach! I never 'eard the like!"

"Sir, I will pay for any losses you have incurred," the Earl snapped, exasperated. "The coach, my good man!"

The assurance of damages had a salutary effect upon the irate villager. "It were big, me lord, as ye know," he said, not giving in entirely. "Yer coachman ought to be clapped up for whippin' up them horses like he did."

The Earl ignored this last remark. "Was there a crest upon the door?" he said.

"Ye mean, the picture smack in the middle of it?"

The Earl sighed. "I do," he said.

" 'Twas a bird, far as I could tell."

"Was it black, with wings spread?"

Mr. Brown scratched his grizzled head. "Could of been," he said. "I don't rightly know. Me cabbages—"

The Earl glanced at Lord Charles. "Lord Chester?" he said.

"It would seem so," Lord Charles agreed.

The footman entered to announce that a third visitor had arrived. "Viscount Shirley, my lord," he said.

"Show him in," the Earl replied.

"I am in," the Viscount grinned, then paused on the threshold in some surprise. "Have I come at an unfortunate time?"

"Not at all," the Earl replied. "We are charmed."

"I have some news for you, but—"

"You are wondering, I think, whether you should now disclose it. You should."

"Be advised, Shirley," Lord Charles interjected,

chuckling. "We seem to be up to our ears in cabbages."

"Jaimie!" the Earl warned in ominous tones.

"Oh, very well," Lord Charles replied, subsiding regretfully.

The Earl turned back to Viscount Shirley. "What have you to tell me of Lottie?" he asked.

"I should first tell you that our little ladybird has been from town. Otherwise, I would have been here sooner."

"I perfectly understand that you would."

"Lottie is a flighty chit. Until I questioned her, she had completely forgotten about the letters. Can you credit that?"

"It would be unexpected, surely."

"Even now, she isn't certain where they are."

"Has she no idea at all?"

"She says she can't recall having seen them after—really, Ravisham, we can't accuse a man purely on Lottie's say-so."

"You are referring to Lord Chester, I apprehend."

Viscount Shirley fairly gaped. "Never say you knew!" he gasped.

The Earl smiled grimly. "Let us say we had deduced it," he said.

"What I want to know," Lord Charles interrupted, "is how he could come by the letters without Lottie's knowing."

"It's quite simple, really," the Earl replied. "Lottie left them lying about, and Chester—er, purloined them."

"You are probably right," Lord Charles agreed. "What will you do now?"

"Go to London immediately. Are you with me?"

"I wouldn't miss it for the world."

"What of you, Shirley?"

"Nothing would give me greater pleasure, but I am on my way to visit my mother. It's her birthday, you know."

"Your pardon, my lord," the Constable said, moving forward. "Could you be more explicit? Who is Lord Chester, and what has he to do with this?"

"Lord Chester is the owner of the coach, and his house in London will be his destination."

"Oh, Lordy!" Mrs. Chittering wailed. "Her ladyship has been taken to the city!"

"You understand the situation, I see," the Earl remarked. "I beg you will not go off into the vapors, Mrs. Chittering. Your mistress will shortly be restored to you."

The Constable's bosom swelled. "I am the law, my lord," he said. "I will accompany you."

"As you wish, Mumfry, but I go by curricle. You will have to ride in the groom's seat up behind."

"I do not mind that, my lord."

"Very well, then, it's settled. Simpson!"

The butler came forward. "Yes, my lord?"

"Send word to the stables to harness the bays to my curricle. No other team, mind. They are the fastest horses I own."

"Very good, my lord."

"You will place two pistols in it. Check their priming yourself."

"Yes, my lord."

"Within fifteen minutes, Simpson."

Mr. Brown sprang forward. "What of me cabbages?" he cried.

The Earl crossed to the door. "Simpson will be charmed to instruct my man of business to pay you for the damned things," he said and went from the room.

Chapter 20

Adrianna, when first hurled down upon the seat of Lord Chester's coach by the blow he had dealt to her head, had lain still, her ears ringing. Nausea threatened to overwhelm her, and for some minutes she lay breathing deeply to overcome a queasiness somewhere in the region of her stomach. By degrees she met with success and was able to struggle to a sitting position and grab for the leather armrest hanging in the corner of the coach. They were moving so fast she found she must cling to it to keep from being tossed against Lord Chester's hateful form. The horses were galloping at a tremendous pace, and she could hear the crack of the coachman's whip urging them on. "We will end in a ditch," she gasped while endeavoring to retain her seat.

When he spoke, Lord Chester's voice was harsh. "Very prettily contrived," he said. "It will, however, avail you nothing. We will not turn over, so put thoughts of escape from your mind."

"Why have you done this, and where are you taking me?"

"You will do better to remain quiet," he shot back, malice in his eyes.

Deducing that he was mad, she turned her head to gaze out of the window in bewilderment, her thoughts in chaos. She scarcely knew the man, having not set eyes on him above twice at some ball or rout. Doubtless he hated her, but why? Perhaps it had something to do with Lord Belderbrock. He had not looked best pleased when she had come across him in his lordship's company. A pretty pair, to be sure! One need only add Grimcoe to the picture for it to be complete. The thought sent a quiver down her spine. Of course, she mused. They were in the blackmailing scheme together. Grimcoe was to secure the letters, while my Lords Chester and Belderbrock would extract payment from their owner, Lord Charles, unless she was much mistaken. There was nothing she

could do, she knew, but to attract as little attention to herself as possible and await her chance.
For she knew she must somehow escape, regardless of the risk.

They came to the outskirts of London with
Adrianna still turning over plans to elude Lord
Chester in her mind. None of them would do,
she knew, feeling downcast. He would not very
easily be gulled. Her brain was feeling numb
when a noisy celebration in the distance caught
her notice. It was made up of singing and laughter and seemed to be coming closer. People in
the streets were turning their heads in the direction of the sound swelling in volume as it approached. Suddenly the coach became surrounded
by a laughing, milling mass of students signaling
the end of term. Lord Chester's coachman swore
loudly and attempted to cleave a path through
the throng, but several of the celebrants clung to
the horses' bridles, thereby nullifying his efforts.
Adrianna saw her chance and took it.

In a twinkling she motioned to a student to
wrench open the door and hurled herself into the
midst of the cheerful mob. Lord Chester lunged
for her to prevent her escape, but, with a speed
born of desperation, she was too quick for him.
The last he saw of her she was being carried along
on the tide by the press of bodies sweeping down
the street like a tidal wave.

The entire merry group swung on down the
broad thoroughfare, their numbers swelling as
they went, until all traffic came to a standstill
and the avenue was theirs. Adrianna glanced

down each side street, and was striving to reach the sidewalk to separate herself from the throng when a hand closed over hers, pulling her along. She clung to it, afraid of losing her footing and being trampled upon, until the laughing student succeeded in pushing his way to the edge of the crowd, with her in tow. Releasing her at the mouth of an alley leading to a labyrinth of winding lanes, he took time to bend his leg in a graceful bow before dashing off in the wake of his companions. Adrianna lost no time in diving into the passage and fleeing down it to the safety of streets too narrow to accommodate the passing of a coach. Aware that people were turning to stare, she slowed to a walk, traversing streets with no idea of where she was or which direction she was headed, until she went around a corner and found herself in a street which looked vaguely familiar. Instinctively she paused, afraid that Lord Chester might somehow have found her out. Relieved that his coach was nowhere in sight, she abandoned the safety of the mews to signal to a hired hackney. Having given its driver the address of Ravisham House, she climbed inside and collapsed upon the seat, weak with relief and knowing she had escaped disaster by no more than a hair's breadth.

A considerable portion of the drive home was taken up in deciding what tale she would spin for the benefit of the servants. Then, philosophically, she shrugged her shoulders. It mattered little what they thought. Rather than become entangled in a morass of lies, she would simply say nothing. She could not, however, help feeling disheveled and slightly ridiculous when the hackney drew up before the house, and she went inside.

Instructing the lone footman found on duty in the hall to send word of her whereabouts to the Earl along with a brief story of her experience, she crossed the vestibule and went upstairs, wanting nothing so much as her bed.

Thus it was that around one hour later, the Earl, tooling his curricle on the road to London at a pace which caused Constable Mumfry to cling to his seat in abject fear, perceived a lackey in the Ravisham livery galloping toward him astride a lathered horse. Pulling up his team, he awaited the servant's arrival with a heavy scowl upon his face. "Why the devil do you mean, riding that animal into the ground?" he demanded the instant the groom drew up beside him.

The groom turned beet red. "Her ladyship sent me, my lord. I—she said—I thought it was urgent."

"Her ladyship!" the Earl uttered. "Where is she?"

"At Ravisham House, my lord."

"Thank God!" he breathed, relieved.

"I told you she would be, old boy," Lord Charles said with a good deal of satisfaction.

The Earl fixed the groom with a stern eye. "You will walk that horse back to town," he said grimly. "Pray to your maker you have not lamed him."

"But—her ladyship seemed so upset, I thought—"

"What do you mean, upset?" the Earl demanded.

"Her ladyship was distraught, my lord. From

having been seized by Lord Chester, and then escaping from him, her ladyship walked for some distance before finding a hackney carriage to bring her home."

"Good God! You never left her alone?"

"No, my lord. I sent for the police to guard the house until your lordship's return."

"It seems I am deeply in your debt. Attend me, however. You will still take good care of your horse. When you have him home safe in the stables, you will perhaps enjoy an unexpected holiday?"

"Yes, sir, my lord," the groom grinned, swinging down from his saddle.

The Earl set his team forward. "Constable Mumfry, you will wish to lead the police in the arrest of Lord Chester, I should imagine."

"I would indeed, my lord," the Constable replied, relieved to see the Earl slowing the pace of his horses. "I imagine we have enough charges against his lordship to send him to the gallows."

"I trust so," the Earl replied. "What will you do now, Jaimie?"

Lord Charles glanced at him somewhat whimsically. "Are you so very anxious to be rid of me?" he said.

The Earl gave a laugh of sheer joy. "May I say I will find you a trifle *de trop?*" he chuckled.

"Have you told Adrianna of my part in this affair?" Lord Charles asked curiously. "I burned the letters, you know."

"You forbade me to tell her, you will remember."

"Well, on second thought, I think she has a right to know."

"If you don't mind, Jaimie, I will—er, use my own discretion in what I tell Adrianna."

As things turned out, he had no need to tell her anything. She told him. Upon the following day. That night, there was no time.

Two hours later he entered her bedroom and shut the door soundlessly. Adrianna was curled up in the middle of the bed, fast asleep with her cheek on her hand. He trod across to her side and stood looking down at her, a tender expression in his eyes. The fire had burned low, but still gave enough light to illuminate her face. Suddenly he sat down upon the bed and pulled her into his arms. "Wake up, dearest," he breathed in her ear. "I have something very pleasant for you."

She opened drowsy eyes and blinked at him. "Oh, is that you, Ivor?" she murmured. "What is it?"

"I love you," he said, kissing her fiercely. "You are my life! Do you hear me?"

"I imagine I do. What time is it?"

"I don't give a damn what time it is. Hide-and-seek! Good God! You frightened me within an inch of my life!"

Before she could think, his lips were on hers and he was kissing her wildly, possessively, demanding a response to his passion, crushing all the breath out of her body. "I will never again let you out of my sight!" he said, raising his head to stare down at her.

Since he palliated this severity by gazing at her with love shining from his eyes, she was undismayed. "Shall you beat me?" she said.

"Yes," he said, pressing her down into the pillows. "But first, I mean to make love to you, my dear and abominable little brat."

Dell Bestsellers

At your local bookstore or use this handy coupon for ordering:

Love—the way you want it!

Candlelight Romances

By the author of <u>Scarlet Shadows</u>

EMMA DRUMMOND

Judith: A proud English beauty, she left the glitter of London society to pursue Alex across two continents.

Hetta: Gentle, tender, she gave her love boldly, without thought of the past or the devastating future that threatened to separate her from Alex forever.

Two women from different worlds, their passions blazed for one man across THE BURNING LAND!

A Dell Book $2.50

Danielle Steel
SUMMER'S END

author of *The Promise*
and *Season of Passion*

As the wife of handsome, successful, inter-
national lawyer Marc Edouard Duras, Deanna
had a beautiful home, diamonds and elegant
dinners. But her husband was traveling between the glamorous capitals of the business
world, and all summer Deanna would be alone.
Until Ben Thomas found her—and laughter
and love took them both by surprise.

A Dell Book $2.50